Balancing Act

Jonathan Plummer

and Karen Hunter

POCKET BOOKS
New York London Toronto Sydney

Pocket Books
A Division of Simon & Schuster, Inc.
1230 Avenue of the Americas
New York, NY 10020

This book is a work of fiction. Names, characters, places, and incidents either are products of the author's imagination or are used fictitiously. Any resemblance to actual events or locales or persons, living or dead, is entirely coincidental.

First Pocket Books paperback edition May 2008

POCKET and colophon are registered trademarks of Simon & Schuster, Inc.

For information about special discounts for bulk purchases, please contact Simon & Schuster Special Sales at 1-800-456-6798 or business@simonandschuster.com.

Designed by Ruth Lee Mui

Manufactured in the United States of America

10 9 8 7 6 5 4 3 2 1

ISBN-13: 978-1-4165-3740-3
ISBN-10: 1-4165-3740-6
ISBN-13: 978-1-4165-3741-0 (pbk)
ISBN-10: 1-4165-3741-4 (pbk)

To all who struggle to find their truth,
their purpose, and themselves

If I didn't define myself for myself, I would be crunched into other people's fantasies for me and eaten alive.

—Audre Lorde

Balancing Act

Chapter One

"You bitch-ass motherfucker!" Tasha Reynolds hauled back as if she was pitching a fastball for the New York Yankees and slapped Justin across the face with all of her might. His head whipped around as a smattering of blood formed where his full lips had crushed into his top teeth.

"Who the fuck do you think you are?! You can't leave me! You ain't going no fucking where!"

If any of Tasha's clients or competitors had seen her, they wouldn't have recognized her. In public, Tasha was one of the most controlled and controlling women there ever was. Tasha was, in every sense of the word, "regal," in her walk, in her talk. She possessed the trained grace of someone with upbringing and character.

She rarely smiled or joked. She was all business and very good at what she did. She was a perfectionist without a conscience. There was no place in her business for someone who was sensitive, for someone who had second thoughts, for someone with emotions.

Tasha Reynolds was at the top of her game because she did what she had to do to be the best. She worked harder than anyone else and she made tough decisions without batting a fake eyelash. She was *never* out of control. She was smooth as ice, cold as ice, hard as ice. Tasha Reynolds always got what she wanted.

And what she wanted right now was Justin Blakeman.

He stood in front of her, wiping the blood from his mouth, trying not to react, holding himself back. The last time a woman had smacked him, he'd been ten years old and it was his mother. He'd lied to her about where he went after school, and she smacked him in the mouth for lying. He also got a beating with a cane when his father got home later that evening. The smack on the mouth by his mother was worse. It was humiliating, even for a ten-year-old. But he'd learned how to take it like a man. And he held himself like a man now.

Justin had been raised in an old-fashioned Jamaican family, where roles were very distinct. Women had their place, and men were king. A man never subjugated himself or bowed to a woman. Justin had allowed himself to be Tasha's subject for far too long, as far as he was concerned. She had been the queen and he had been part of her royal world. He had allowed himself to be paraded around like one of those Westminster Kennel Club show dogs for three years, at her beck and call, doing whatever she asked. He'd loved her in the beginning, and there was a part of him that would love her always. But now he was reclaiming his manhood.

"It's over, Tasha," he said as calmly as he could, trying not to respond at all to her emotional outrage. His nonreaction stoked her anger.

"It will *never* be over until I say it's over!" she growled.

Justin turned and began to leave. He had packed one bag, taking only the few clothes he'd bought for himself and some personal items that he'd brought with him from Jamaica. He knew how she was and he didn't want to give her any cause to come after him.

As Justin reached for the door, a Baccarat ashtray narrowly missed his head, crashing into the cedar door. It didn't shatter, the crystal was too heavy. But had it connected with his head, Justin would have had at least a concussion, if not worse.

"Where the *fuck* do you think you're going?! Are you hard of hearing? It's *not* over, Justin!"

Tasha rushed him, slapping at his face and shredding the skin on his forearms with her nails as she tried to pry his bag out of his hand. He dropped the bag and grabbed her arms, stopping her from hitting and scratching him. She was struggling and he threw her to the floor. But Tasha was possessed. She kept coming at him, swinging. He blocked most of her blows and grabbed her around the waist, lifted her from the ground, and carried her to the couch in the living room, throwing her like a rag doll.

"Now, stop this!" he said, finally raising his voice. "Look at yourself, Tasha! This isn't you! It doesn't have to end like this! Just let me go!"

Tasha's chest was heaving. She was out of breath and going out of her mind. She rushed him one more time. This time Justin met her with a blow to her head, driving her backward with force. She fell to the ground hard, teetering on the verge of consciousness.

"You motherfucker!" she slurred. "You . . . you're going to pay for this."

Justin looked at her—a woman the world saw as untouchable greatness. He looked at her with sadness. He walked calmly to the door, picked up his bag, and left. He didn't look back. He walked to the elevator and rode the twenty floors down, collecting his thoughts. His black Lexus convertible—the car she'd bought him—was parked in the front of the garage, as it always was. A nice, fast drive was just what the doctor ordered.

Justin started the engine and screeched out of the garage, headed for the FDR Drive and on to his new life.

He was excited. He was free. More free than his days chopping sugarcane in Jamaica. Freer than he had ever been in his life. He allowed himself to smile, dabbing away a bit of the ugliness he had just left behind, as he thought about where he was headed next. It would be the first official night as a single man. He was free to love. And he couldn't wait.

He selected "Love Songs" on his iPod's playlist and drank in the opening notes of Maxwell's "Till the Cops Come Knockin'."

Gonna take you in the room suga'
Lock you up and love for days . . .

Justin was caught up in the music. And caught up in his fantasies. He didn't notice the flashing lights bearing down on him and he raced past the Twenty-first Street exit. He was a couple of miles from Tasha in distance and a million miles from her in his mind. But it was all catching up with him.

"Pull over!" The gruff voice came over the loudspeaker, shaking Justin out of his mist. He'd never noticed the sirens because

Maxwell's song has sirens throughout, which he had grown used to over the years.

"Pull over, now!"

Justin eased over.

"What the . . . ?" But he knew. "Tasha."

The police were angry for having to chase him for nearly a mile. They got out, hands on their guns, one at the passenger-side window, the other at the driver's side.

"Step out of the car," the officer barked.

"What? Why did you pull me over, Officer?" Justin asked.

"Shut up and step out of the car!"

Justin kept his hands in full sight. He was new to America, but he'd heard about Amadou Diallo and Sean Bell and knew he was black enough to give a New York police officer cause to pause. He didn't want to be that kind of victim. So he kept his hands raised above his head and, because he didn't want any trouble, asked the officer to open the door.

The officer opened the door with one hand and yanked Justin out of the car with the other hand, threw him to the ground, and handcuffed him.

"You have the right to remain silent . . ."

Chapter Two

Three years earlier

Justin Blakeman peeled the shirt from his sticky body, looking for one dry spot to use to wipe the salty sweat from his face. It was pouring from his brow into his eyes, making them beet red as the sun beat down on him with its hundred-degree temperature. He had been on the road from Kingston to Ocho Rios for three hours and had had about a dozen sales. Justin was satisfied. He had planned on staying out there for two more hours before calling it a day.

Justin couldn't find a dry spot on his shirt, so he simply twisted his gray cotton T-shirt like a rag, wringing the sweat out, and wiped off his face, his chest, and his arms. He was dripping. But he loved it. He loved the sweat of a hard day's work. He put his wet, sweaty shirt in his back pocket, most of it hanging out, and waited for his next customer.

Selling sugarcane on the streets wasn't what he'd imagined when he'd asked to be a part of the family business. The Blakemans owned one of the largest farms on the island of Jamaica. Cane was their biggest crop. They also owned a refinery where the cane was made into rum. Justin's uncle ran the refinery, while his father ran the farm. It was a business started by Justin's grandfather in the early 1920s. Justin's father wanted his son to know the business from the ground up, and he meant it literally.

"Son, your grandfather started this business with this land and with his hands," his father told him when Justin asked him about getting into the business. "And if a Blakeman expects to inherit this land, he will have to roll up his sleeves and work the land, just as your grandfather did, just as I did."

Justin had an option. He could go to the university. But he didn't have much interest in furthering his education. While Justin wasn't quite sure what he wanted, he knew for sure he didn't want to go back to school. He'd spent too many years in private school learning about British history and literature, calculus and chemistry, and a bunch of other subjects he never expected to use in real life. Working—now that was real life. Being in that snooty private school with all of those stuck-up rich kids didn't sit well with Justin. He looked forward to reconnecting with his roots.

Justin's family claimed to be descendants of Queen Nanny of the Maroons. Legend had it that after Nanny was brought to Jamaica in the hold of a slave ship from Africa's Gold Coast to work on a sugarcane plantation, she helped lead a revolt. Slaves on her plantation won their freedom and founded a community high up in the mountains above Kingston, in Portland. Those slaves had hundreds of acres of land. Today there is still a section of town named Nanny Town, after Queen Nanny of the Maroons.

She died in the 1730s and reportedly had no children, but that didn't stop many from claiming her as their matriarch. The Blakemans were certainly part of the Maroon community, a group of proud Jamaicans who had continuously stood up to European rule and fought for their freedom. Justin's family used that slave land to build wealth and stature. His grandfather turned that land into a moneymaker.

Working that land for Justin was liberating because he was doing it on his terms. He didn't make a lot of money growing sugarcane and selling it on the roads of his town, but he enjoyed it. And the money would be there. He was a Blakeman. He came from money, and he would inherit money. But the experiences he had on the land and on the streets of Jamaica were priceless. Justin loved the smell of the earth, all of the fascinating insects and worms that he would encounter. He loved watching the cane grow from a seed into this strong, bamboolike weed that seemed to grow so quickly he could barely keep up. He loved chopping it down and getting that first sweet taste. The sweetest part was toward the bottom of the stalk.

Working that land had some other positive effects.

Justin's hands were strong, his forearms like corded steel. He didn't have just a six-pack. Every single possible abdominal muscle was uniquely defined, from the oblique to the little section at his pubic region. From the bending and stretching, the chopping and hauling of the cane he had a body that could never be built in a gym. It was strong from the inside out and there wasn't a machine in Gold's Gym that could duplicate the kind of movement and weight training and conditioning that Justin put himself through.

He was as proud of his body as he was about who he was.

That body. That was the first thing Tasha Reynolds noticed when she pulled her rental car over to the side of the road where Justin stood with his cane.

"Oh shit," she muttered to herself, pulling her Gucci frames down her nose to get a better look. As head of her own New York City modeling agency, Tasha had seen the most beautiful bodies and faces the world had to offer. She'd worked in the industry for more than fifteen years and seen the likes of Naomi and Tyra, and Giselle, Marcus, Tyson, and Ashton go from no-names to household faces with movie deals, television talk shows, and billboards in the middle of Times Square. But this specimen was something else. Tasha knew instantly that he would be a star.

"How much for the cane?" she said after rolling down her window. She needed to hear him talk. She needed to see his face up close. If his mannerisms weren't right, she could buy her cane and keep on moving.

Tasha loved discovering "new" talent. That was her forte. She was careful not to get caught up in just a pretty face or a tight body. Studying her subject was important. One time, she'd been in the Bank of America in New York and had seen a beautiful specimen of a young man. He was barely twenty, with perfectly groomed locks. His skin was chocolate coated and blemish free. She could tell he worked out, even under his heavy jeans and oversize shirt. Tasha had X-ray vision when it came to that. She could tell not only if the body was solid, but also which muscle group needed more work, just with one glance. This boy didn't need any work. But before she approached him, she watched him for a few minutes.

First, he ran his fingers through his locks and smelled the tips of his fingers. He did this three or four times. She was about to overlook that, but then he took his index finger and ran it behind his ear and smelled that, too. That was it.

He's just damn nasty, she thought.

That young man didn't know how close he'd been to actually being "discovered." Tasha wanted to spend a little time with Mr. Perfect Jamaican; she needed to study him to see if he had any weird, disgusting ticks, any hygiene issues, any missing teeth.

"How much?" Tasha asked again.

"How much do you want to pay?" Justin said, smiling coyly, baring the most perfect, straight white teeth that played off his rich dark brown skin.

"Oh, you're a playful one," she said. "How about if I said I wanted to pay nothing?"

"Well, then, I would have to remind you that, in this world, you get nothing for nothing," he said, the accent a mix of island patois and the queen's English. His private school speech classes always came through.

"Okay, I got a better offer for you," she said.

"Now, lady, I don't even know you. What kind of man do I look like?"

"Oh, please, don't flatter yourself!" said Tasha. She didn't crack a smile. She wanted him to know that sex was the furthest thing from her mind. "Young man, I *am* interested in your body. But it's strictly business!"

Tasha pulled out one of her modeling agency cards and handed it to him.

"I want you to come to New York," she said. "I have a job offer for you."

Justin looked puzzled.

"In case you haven't noticed, I already *have* a job," he said.

"A *real* job," Tasha said. "Turn around."

"I'm not turning around. I'm not going to New York with you. Now do you want this cane or not?" said Justin, getting annoyed.

Tasha smiled. Playing hard to get, huh? she thought. She knew he was *going* to show her everything she wanted to see and he was *going* to go back to New York with her. Tasha never took no for an answer and she always got what she wanted.

"Look, I'm leaving this island in three days. So you have that long to think about my offer. It's a once-in-a-lifetime opportunity. I will make you a star. And until I do, I will be footing the bill. You will want for nothing. My cell phone number is on the back of my card. You have three days to make up your mind."

Tasha handed Justin a five-dollar bill and took the cane that she had no intention of eating.

"Keep the change," she said as she rolled up her window, put the air-conditioning on High, and drove off.

Justin was annoyed, a little miffed, and, at the same time, spellbound.

He wanted to crumple the card and toss it, but instead he looked at. He was going to put it in his back pocket—the one without the shirt—but was afraid that the sweat might smear the ink of the cell phone number she'd written on the back. Justin had already made up his mind that he was *not* going to call her. But he wanted to keep the card intact, just in case.

Just in case . . .

In his mind's eye

Who does she think she is? That superior attitude, as if she's coming in here to rescue someone. Like she's in Africa, saving a starving child. Who does she think she is? Angelina Jolie? Madonna? Fuck that.

Do I look like I have flies on my eyeballs and a protruding stomach? Those damn Americans. Every year they come to this island with their shit.

"Yah, mon, where can I get some weed?"

I get stopped at least a dozen times with that one. And if it's not thinking that every fucking body in Jamaica smokes weed, then it's thinking every man will fuck your brains out. That damn woman with her book ruined it for us—now all we get are these women thinking they can get their groove back.

And my people, my people—they haven't helped dispel any of those myths. Most even perpetuate them. But I can't be the one. I can't follow behind this arrogant woman to New York. To be a model? *Come on now!*

Still . . .

Maybe it would be exciting. To be in New York, with all of that craziness. I always thought I'd go there on holiday before working at the refinery next year. But how would it be to go there like this?

And there is definitely something intriguing about that lady. I can't put my finger on it. As infuriating as she is with that sense of entitlement, there is something vulnerable about her that I like.

My parents will lose their minds. They are expecting me to apprentice with my uncle at the refinery in the fall and learn that part of the business. They may even disinherit me.

Wait a minute. What am I thinking? There is no way that I'm going to New York with that woman to be a model. Let me just focus on selling the rest of this cane, getting home, taking a long, hot shower, cracking open a Heineken, *and relaxing.*

Let me get back to reality and something real. Because that other thing is just crazy.

Still . . .

Who the fuck is *that woman, really?!*

Chapter Three

Tasha couldn't remember the last time she'd been this affected by any man. But she was absolutely blown away by Justin Blakeman. It wasn't just his body—which was perfection. Michelangelo's *David* couldn't hold a candle to it. It was his attitude. Tasha had yet to meet a man who could resist her; not only that, she had yet to meet a male or female who, when presented with an opportunity to be a star, wouldn't jump at it. Justin wasn't nonchalant or aloof. He was defiant and determined—two qualities she knew would earmark him for stardom.

American Idol and other reality shows took off because everyone wants, everyone demands, their fifteen minutes of fame—whether they deserve it (and most don't) or not. Tasha had offered

Justin the opportunity of a lifetime and he'd taken her card as if she had handed him a dog biscuit.

"Oh, he is *so* coming back to New York!" Tasha said out loud to herself—because she knew it. She knew it like she knew her name. She knew it—just as she'd known the day she left that modeling agency after one last rejection that she would be back, and with a vengeance.

Tasha Reynolds had come to New York to be a model. She was six feet tall and had a body that rivaled Janet Jackson's—the in-shape, 2001-concert-ready Janet Jackson. She was a head turner. Tasha had flawless skin and almond-shaped eyes with huge irises. You could barely see any of the whites around them. Looking into Tasha's eyes was like getting lost in a dark forest. And she knew how to use them. Her stare was intense, so much so that she could intimidate anyone with just one look.

Tasha was also known to rock various lace-front wigs in all colors and cuts, which gave her an air of unpredictability. It kept people around her on their toes. But Tasha's biggest selling point was her personality, which was a mix of Grace Jones and Martha Stewart. She was outspoken and outrageous and all business. Behind her back they called her the Ice Queen, but they could have called her that to her face, because it fit. Tasha got wind of the nickname and liked it. She was cold, hard, and smooth, like ice. And she was definitely a queen.

Cultivated royalty. Cultivated the way Marguerite Johnson had gotten out of that cage, found her voice, and re-created herself in the form of Maya Angelou. Cultivated the way Anna Mae Bullock coached the country out of herself to become Tina Turner. Cultivated the way Eartha Mae Kitt, born on a South Carolina plantation in abject poverty, obliterated all traces of her early beginnings to become an international superstar with a purrrrrfectly regal accent.

Like Oprah Winfrey, born in Kosciusko, Mississippi, Tasha Reynolds had found a way to incorporate the charm of her southern roots, but completely erase all traces of backwoods and country. For Maya, Tina, Eartha, and Oprah, the transformation was otherwordly. Almost like the phoenix, they rebuilt themselves out of the ashes of their broken, harsh, violent, and abusive lives. It was as if their hardships gave them the material for greatness.

The same was true of Tasha.

Just about every night little Tasha Reynolds cried herself to sleep. She hoped her tears might drown out the noise coming from the bedroom right next to hers. It was becoming routine. Every night Joseph Reynolds would come home late. Tasha's mother, Tamara, would question him about his whereabouts and that would start it.

"Bitch, who the fuck do you think you're talking to?" Joseph would start. "I am a grown motherfucking man! You don't ask me shit!"

"I am your wife," Tamara would respond. "I have a right to know where you've been and what you're doing!"

"You don't have a right to nothing but to keep this motherfucking house clean, take care of my baby girl, and fuck me when I want it!" he would say, the insults increasing in intensity. Each "bitch" and nasty word felt like a whip across Tasha's back. She couldn't understand how her father could be so cruel at night, behind a closed door when he thought no one was listening, and so wonderful in the daytime.

Joseph Reynolds seemed to have a split personality. Tamara sometimes wished he would just beat her mother so the cops would come—maybe that would be enough for her mother to finally leave. But he never did hit her. The words were actually worse. They were demeaning and they chipped away at Tasha's respect for both of her parents—her father for doing it and her mother for taking it.

Tasha would roll her eyes on the occasion when her parents would entertain. Her father had to have everything just right—fresh cut flowers, the perfect meal that her mother had to cook—all to impress his fraternity brothers with their trophy wives. During those times, Tasha had to stay in her room. As her girth was growing, she had become an embarrassment. He never said anything to Tasha's face, but she heard him yelling at her mother one night about how fat she had allowed Tasha to get.

"What the fuck are you trying to create here?" he said. "How fat is she going to get?"

Joseph made it his business to never say a harsh word in front of his daughter, ever. He wanted his daughter to think he was the perfect daddy. And from the outside he *was* perfect—six-foot-three, handsome, clean-shaven, corporate job, bringing home six figures, nice-sized house, latest model BMW in the two-car garage. In this little town of Augusta, Georgia, a town rich with another kind of tradition when it came to blacks, Joseph Reynolds was a bit of a standout. He had definitely "made it."

He even doted on his daughter. Joseph would always have hugs and kisses for Tasha. It was the ultimate conflict. She loved her daddy dearly. But she also hated the man with a passion. She hated how phony he was. She hated how he treated her mother—how he pretended to love her because she fit the right image. What

Joseph loved was power and control. He used his money to dominate and break Tasha's mother.

Tamara didn't work. She forfeited her freedom for a life she thought she wanted and she was miserable. She took her misery out on her only child. Tamara was jealous of the relationship Tasha had with her father. She was also jealous of Tasha's choices. Most mothers want the best for their children. Tamara subconsciously wanted someone to feel worse than she did.

So Tasha began to eat to cover up the pain of knowing that her perfect family was one big lie. In her ten-year-old mind, Tasha somehow knew how helpless, powerless, and miserable she was. But the food gave her some control. So she ate. She ate and she cried.

Tasha also hated her mother for being so weak.

"Why does she stay with him and take it?" she would ask herself. "I will never allow anybody to control me like that!"

But Tasha had no voice. So she let food become her voice. It was her spokesperson. She ate and waited until she had her chance to really control her own destiny. Until then she exercised the only control she had.

By the time Tasha reached the age of twelve, she was pushing 220 pounds, had a face full of pimples, and no friends.

She also carried the anger around inside and wouldn't open up to anyone. Her only saving grace was that she was good in school. Bringing home A's kept her parents from bothering her too much. They were too busy dealing with their own problems, and as long as Tasha was successful in school, that meant they didn't have to expend any energy on her.

Tasha's mother tried to get her to control her weight. She would torture her once a month with shopping trips. That was when Tasha became interested in fashion. She and her mother would shop at the mall and she would be dragged into Lane Bryant.

Tasha wanted to shop at the Gap, Aéropostale, and Urban Outfitters. She wanted to wear BCBG, Citizens of Humanity, Polo, and the other styles that kids in her school were sporting.

"Baby, those jeans don't go up to size twenty-two," her mother would remind her. "You have to buckle down and lose weight if you want me to buy you some Gap jeans, sweetie. It's just that simple."

Tasha hated that bitch Lane Bryant, whoever she was. She hated her for her cheap, Lycra-infused pants, her big, ugly floral-print shirts. Lane Bryant had tried to get "hip," but for a twelve-year-old there was nothing hip about wearing the Lane Bryant label on your ass. It wasn't cool. She didn't want to look like Mo'Nique.

Standing in the fitting room, looking at the muffin top spill out over the size-22 Lane Bryant jeans, Tasha made up her mind right then to make a change.

"You have such a pretty face. You have so much potential, baby," her mother said. "You might need a twenty-four. I'll go get you a bigger size."

Oh, hell no! Tasha thought. She was not going to wear a size 24. She was done. Tasha had begun reading books by Judith Krantz. They opened her mind to possibilities she didn't know existed. They awakened things inside her body that she had no clue were there. Tasha wanted to know what that love feeling was like. She wasn't getting any at home. She knew there was something more out there. Maybe her mother had a point. She was only eating herself into oblivion to spite her parents. But outside the weight issue, neither of them seemed to care much. So who was she hurting, really?

Tasha would spend hours in her room reading. And when she wasn't reading, she was watching old Katharine Hepburn movies and Bette Davis movies and Joan Crawford movies. She admired those women—their glamour, the way they spoke, their strength. She studied their speech patterns. She also loved Diahann Carroll, the first real black diva of Tasha's time. Even though Tasha was such a little girl when Dominique Deveraux burst on the scene in the mid to late 1980s on *Dynasty,* Tasha was spellbound. Dominique was so much more than either Krystal or Alexis Carrington because Dominique looked like Tasha . . . or at least the way Tasha imagined she should look.

By the time Tasha turned twelve, she had perfected the unaccented, perfect diction and grammar of the small- and big-screen divas she grew up idolizing. Heading into her teens, Tasha was caught up in fashion. She would take the money her father gave her and spend it on fashion magazines. She would tear out the pictures of the models and tape them to her wall. She was just a baby when Beverly Johnson made her groundbreaking appearance on the cover of *Vogue* in 1974, but Tasha became a quick study. She also followed the career of Iman Abdulmajid, the daughter of a Somali ambassador to Saudi Arabia who became a modeling sensation in America and was known by only her first name. She was excited when Alek Wek came on the scene because she looked so different from anyone she had ever seen on the runway or on the pages of magazines—outside *National Geographic,* of course.

If *she* can be a model, hell, anyone can be a model, she thought, looking at her pictures.

Alek was striking, but also startlingly ugly by most standards—especially in the black community, where skin color and hair texture and length were so much a part of determining beauty. Alek was blaaaaaack, bald headed, nappy headed, and bony.

But Tasha felt ugly, too. So seeing Alek gave her a glimmer of hope.

On that last tortured shopping trip to Lane Bryant, Tasha made a decision. She *would* fit into the clothes she wanted to wear. She found a way. When she turned fifteen, Tasha discovered that if she simply threw up everything she ate, she could lose lots of weight. By the summer of her sixteenth birthday, Tasha had lost eighty-two pounds. She was six feet, a hundred and thirty-seven pounds and ready to take on the world.

By her seventeenth birthday, she'd made a decision. She had saved up more than $2,000. She took her money and bought a one-way bus ticket to New York City. She left Augusta determined to be the next Beverly Johnson. She had done her homework. Tasha had studied all of the agencies, knew all of the top agents and all of the other players in the game. She would get to New York and go on the rounds. She figured she would be signed in a couple of weeks and then she would be off to Paris to do runway modeling. She had it all planned out.

Unfortunately, when she got to New York, she was told the same thing over and over: "You don't have the right look."

"What the fuck does that mean?" she said to the white-bread agent at Wilhelmina, the fifth agency that told her that.

"Um, well," the woman stammered, taken aback by Tasha's boldness. "We're looking for models that are, well, a little less hippy."

"Hippy? I barely have hips. What are you talking about?"

Tasha said. She was right. The one thing she didn't have was hips. She was actually pretty boyish in that department.

"Well, it's not hips, exactly. It's your derriere. It's too large," said the agent, satisfied that she'd just spit it out.

"My ass is too big?!" Tasha said. "You have got to be kidding!"

Her ass was too big. Tyra Banks had not yet come on the scene to let the world know that curves are part of what makes a woman a woman. They weren't ready for Tasha, who at six feet had a body that rivaled Janet's, but had Janet's ass, too. With all that hard work Tasha had put in to be ready, it was not enough.

She starved herself, losing more weight than she should and it still wasn't enough. She'd left her home in Georgia because she *knew* she was going to be a model and yet that door kept closing in her face. There were no friends or allies or mentors for Tasha in New York, no one to turn to. She had to find a job to support herself—and fast. Two thousand dollars wasn't going to last very long in New York.

She took a position as an assistant to an agent at Wilhelmina. The white-bread agent liked Tasha's "spunk." She also felt a little bad about turning her down. There was an assistant's position open and she offered it to Tasha.

"You can learn the business," the white-bread lady told Tasha. "Who knows, maybe the industry will change in a year or two and your type will be coveted. This business is funny like that."

Tasha didn't think shit was funny. But she decided to take the job. She needed to take care of herself. There was no way Tasha was going back to Augusta. She just couldn't. She figured she *would* learn the business of modeling from the bottom to the top, and when she learned all she needed, they had better watch out. She would be back.

It took Tasha two years of intense learning, and even more intense saving. But Tasha Reynolds came back to give the modeling agencies, and all of those who'd said her booty was too big, something to regret.

Tasha started her own agency.

In less than three years, she built hers into one of the top modeling agencies in the business. She even managed to steal away Elite's top female model and discovered Dorian Vance, who was on the billboard for Abercrombie & Fitch right before the entrance into the Lincoln Tunnel.

And with this new find, Justin Blakeman, Tasha would solidify herself as the queen of the modeling world.

"He's coming back with me to New York," she announced to herself. "He is mine."

Chapter Four

The drive up Naggo Head seemed like the longest drive Justin had ever made. His palms were sweaty as he gripped the wheel of the Land Rover his parents had bought him for his high school graduation four years before. As he drew closer to the family home, his heart began to beat faster.

"How am I going to tell them this?"

Justin's reputation among the Blakeman family was as the one who never made waves. He was a good kid who did what he was told and never got into trouble. He did relatively well in school and didn't have a string of girls coming and going. In fact, Justin had only one serious girlfriend, Nannette—at least the only one his family ever got to know. Her father was in politics and she came from money, too. Everyone thought Justin was going to ask her to marry him when they graduated. And he might have, until he caught this girl with proper breeding on her knees after school in the dean's office, giving the assistant headmaster head.

The headmaster had asked Justin if he would locate Mr. Fellows for an after-school meeting. To this day, Justin doesn't know why he didn't knock, which would have been the appropriate thing to do. He doesn't know why he just barged in. But what he saw was devastating. Nannette was his first love.

It took Justin a long time to recover. Maybe he never had. Maybe he was still a little gun-shy. That's why he'd only dated casually since Nannette. She'd tried to win him back, giving him some lame excuse about being coerced by Fellows, who threatened to give her detention if she didn't comply. But Justin wasn't buying it. It didn't make any sense.

He never told his parents what had happened. They kept asking, "Why aren't you with Nannette anymore?" He would simply say, "It just didn't work out." They didn't press him because Justin was always levelheaded. If he made a decision, it was usually the right one. If Nannette wasn't around, there was probably a good reason.

Justin never did do anything unless there was a good reason. Now he was going to tell his parents that he was leaving Jamaica, heading for New York—but this time he had no good reason. He'd met some woman on the road who'd told him she would make him a star. This was not going to be an easy sell.

The phone call he'd made the night before to Tasha Reynolds was brief and inconclusive. He didn't confirm that he was actually leaving.

"This is the cane seller you met on the road," Justin said after Tasha said hello. No niceties, no pleasantries. If this is business, Justin thought, then let it be business. "So, when do you plan on leaving?"

"I will be here three more days," said Tasha, as curt as Justin. "If you plan on coming with me, I expect you to meet me at the airport at three on Friday. My flight leaves at five."

"I'll let you know something by tomorrow," Justin said. " 'Bye."

They hung up, but Justin had already made up his mind. Now he had to somehow convince his family that this would be the opportunity of a lifetime. It wasn't about the stardom or the modeling, because Justin really didn't know what that would entail. The idea of pouting his mouth, posing, and looking like that character from *Zoolander* didn't really appeal to him. It was about the possibility of possibilities—it was about exploring what could be.

He knew the life that was waiting for him in Jamaica: He was going to head up an empire. He was going to get married, have a couple of kids—hopefully, one of them would be a boy who would be groomed to carry on the family business. That was the plan he was on track to follow.

But before settling into that existence, Justin thought to himself, Why not? Why not do something a little different? Why not go outside the norm and do something a little bit crazy? If it didn't work out, he could—and would—simply come back home and live out the life that was set for him. But before making that lifelong commitment, he decided it was time to have a little bit of fun.

He'd watched his father, Bertrand, follow in the family tradition. Although he had everything, Bertrand Bateman was restless and unhappy. Maybe that's why he had a woman in just about every province. He was rarely home, always out on "business"—which was usually some sort of monkey business with a woman.

He wasn't home when Justin pulled up to the gate, punched in the password, and drove around the circular drive. He parked on the side so that he could enter from the kitchen. Cherry Gardens was just a notch below Beverly Hills—a small notch. Yes, Jamaica had its very own Beverly Hills and it was just as opulent. There were palatial estates, with their swimming pools—indoor and out, tennis courts, three or four maids and other "staff," and Bentleys in the cobblestone drives.

A small notch. Actually, many of the island's wealthy lived in Cherry Gardens, in the St. Catherine's province, because it was quaint, residential, and family oriented. Justin grew up barely knowing about the poverty that plagued most of Kingston and the violence and crime that accompanied it.

His home was a haven, guarded by gates and three Donnerberg rottweilers—three of the most lovable yet vicious dogs ever made. He was picked up and dropped off every day from his prestigious school. He had a live-in maid, a swimming pool, and all of the trimmings.

Justin was isolated from the real world—a world his parents wanted him never to experience. But now Justin was going headlong into a world even more dangerous than the one they were protecting him from in Jamaica. He was going to New York City with a perfect stranger. He was exhilarated.

He came into the kitchen, with its imported Italian marble floors and granite counters and rich oak cabinets. The smell of escoveitch fish hit his nostrils. He could always expect a pot of something to be simmering on the stove. His grandmother, who lived with them, loved to cook—bammy, stew chicken, plantains (the best he'd ever tasted), callaloo—and Justin loved to eat.

When Justin walked into the open kitchen, his ma-ma was standing over her pot. He walked up behind her and gave her a bear hug.

"How's my favorite lady?" Justin said, practically lifting her from the ground.

Justin's grandmother was all of five feet one—more than a foot and an inch shorter than Justin. She was a tiny woman with a strong spirit. His mother's mother had come to live with them after his maternal grandfather died, when Justin was fifteen. He loved having her there, not just for her cooking skills, but for the kernels of wisdom she always supplied. His ma-ma didn't speak much, but when she did, it was exactly what needed to be said.

If she was on Justin's side, it would be a lot easier to get his parents to go along.

"What are you doing here?" his grandmother said. "I didn't expect you until Sunday, for family night."

"Well, Ma-Ma, that's why I'm here now," Justin said. "I don't think I'll be here on Sunday. I am thinking about going away on a little adventure."

Justin tried to make it sound mysterious and exciting, but concern etched itself across his grandmother's face. She washed her hands, then grabbed a thick white terry towel to dry them off, taking a seat at the kitchen island.

"What's this adventure you're talking about?"

"I have a great opportunity, Ma-Ma, a once-in-a-lifetime opportunity, and I need you to support me on this." Justin reverted back to being a little boy. He felt like he was seven years old again and in trouble. Back then he would run to his grandmother to rescue him. She always did. She was the one to stand in front of him when his mother came after him with the cane or a belt.

"Don't you hit that boy," Ma-Ma would say. "You know he's a good boy. Your beating him will not teach him a thing. Talk to him. Find out why he did it."

Justin was the kind of kid who could be reasoned with and talked to. He didn't need to be beaten. Ma-Ma didn't have to step in often at all. But Justin knew there was at least one person in his life who would always stand up for him.

"I met this woman . . . an executive. She owns a modeling agency in New York . . . she says she can make me a star," Justin stammered.

"A star? Is that what you want? You want to be a star?"

"I want to see," Justin said. "I want to know if, if I can be one."

Ma-Ma looked at him with a doubtful twist to her mouth.

"Hmmm. I don't think you want to be a star at all. I don't see it."

"What, do you have a lie-detector test under that dress?" Justin said, making a broad smile cross his grandmother's face. "Ma-Ma, I will have so much on me in a few years. And I want to see what's out there. I want to have no regrets when I settle down and take care of my duty. I don't want to look back on this moment and wish I had at least seen what the possibilities were. If it doesn't work out, I'll be back soon. But I have nothing to lose."

"Well, I wouldn't quite say that." Ma-Ma brought a voice of reason to the table. "You don't know this woman. What if she's lying to you? I know you're a man, Jussy. But you're not worldly. You are so young. You don't know the evils of this world. This woman could be setting you up. How do you know? You could have a *lot* to lose."

"I hear you, Ma-Ma. I just feel that she's telling the truth. I know she is. You have to trust that I have some discernment, that you taught me a little something over the years."

"Well . . . I trust you, Jussy. I do. I just want you to be careful. So who is this woman?"

"Her name is Tasha Reynolds. I already Googled her. She's legitimate. She has ten models—six are some of the top models in the world. She saw me selling cane by the roadside and she said I could be a star. Now you know I don't care about that, but to be in New York, with someone like that, and get to see another kind of life, at least for a little while, will be an experience, don't you think?"

"Yes, baby, I do. But it doesn't matter what I think. You know your parents have plans for you. And those plans don't include running off to New York to be a model."

"That's why you're going to help me convince them," Justin said, grabbing his ma-ma around the waist and giving her a playful hug.

"Ahhh. So you're using me, huh? Oh no, my boy, you are on your own with this one. You want to be a big man and run off to the States? Well, this is your first step. You have to face your parents. You have to tell them this by yourself."

Justin faked a pout. But he also knew he was never alone. Ma-Ma would be there for him, as she always was.

Chapter Five

Two glasses of champagne awaited Justin and Tasha as they took their plush leather seats right behind the cockpit, in first class. Justin sat near the window; he wanted to drink it all in. He was jittery, and couldn't keep still in his seat. This was his first plane ride. Justin's cousins and even his dad had been to "the States"—which always meant either Florida or New York. But Justin had visited only in his dreams.

He had always planned to go to the United States when he graduated from college. In fact, his family had promised him a trip. But he decided not to even go to college. He figured he would get there soon enough. Florida was not on his to-do list. It seemed like a lesser version of the paradise he lived in. Aside from what he'd heard about South Beach, Miami, and its beautiful people and off-the-hook nightlife—Justin was never a big party person—there wasn't much Florida could offer.

He had access to a private beach not too far from his home. And the water was much cleaner.

But New York was another story. Justin had had a secret, long-distance love affair with New York ever since his dad brought him back a souvenir of the Empire State Building, enclosed in one of those water-filled plastic domes that you can shake and have it snow over the city.

"What's that white stuff?" eight-year-old Justin had asked his father after shaking the dome vigorously, watching the white flakes slowly settle to the bottom.

"That's snow," his dad answered.

"What's snow?"

Justin's father took him to the encyclopedia and showed him. The tiny ice flakes that could coat an entire city or bury an entire town fascinated Justin. He saw snowmen and snowballs. Then he turned to the section in his encyclopedia on New York City and his whole world opened. He read everything he could on New York, with its huge skyscrapers and millions of people—oh, the fast-moving, fast-talking people.

He imagined this tiny island of Manhattan—only thirteen miles long and two and a half miles wide—packed down with as many as eight million people at any one time. How was that possible? He had caught the New Year's Eve celebration in Times Square on television once and wished he could be right in the middle of that screaming mob.

Jamaica was 146 miles by 51 miles at its widest point. Downtown Kingston at times seemed too crowded. He couldn't imagine

New York. Now he was going to be there. Tasha had promised that she would make him the toast of New York.

Sitting on the plane, sipping champagne, Justin thought about leaving Jamaica, where he was being groomed for greatness. His future was planned for him. He had roots, solid roots, and a bright future. His family was among the wealthiest on the island. He had access to money. And soon he would have all of that money—the only son to the largest rum distiller in Jamaica. Justin had a built-in career that would afford him not just money, but also prestige. If he chose, at some point, it would not be out of the question to see himself as prime minister. He had the pedigree. He had the clean background. He had the looks. He was fine—Morris Chestnut, Tyson Beckford, Djimon Hounsou, young Sidney Poitier kind of fine. And it seemed as if every woman of a certain caliber—and beyond—was positioning herself to be Mrs. Justin Blakeman. It was a strange place to be for Justin, who seemed to run away from the attention most men would simply bask in.

Ever since he could remember, Justin had been at the center of some female attention. His first sexual experience had happened when he was very young. The Blakemans had a Dominican maid who had been working for the family for three months. She was in her early twenties and she was very curious about Justin, who was a very shy, gangly kid who spent most of his time alone and in his room. Maritza could see the potential. Actually, she noticed the thickness bulging through his shorts—and he wasn't even aroused—and she was hungry to see it up close. Maritza was a closet freak. She cracked that closet door open one afternoon when an unsuspecting Justin came down to the kitchen for a snack.

Ma-Ma was taking a nap and Maritza seized the moment. She lured Justin into the laundry room, just off the kitchen, and locked

"Did you want to kill your poor grandmother!" his mother yelled. "You could have given her a heart attack. You are a Blakeman! You know better than that. If you didn't before, you do now."

His father finally stepped in.

"Eveline, I think the boy understands. Don't you, Justin?" his father said, with a sheepish grin on his face that he tried to hide from his angry wife.

"Yes, sir," Justin said, just above a whisper.

He understood well. He understood that what he did was very acceptable in the eyes of his father. But he must make sure that next time he should not get caught. That was the understanding. Justin's father was known throughout the island as a ladies' man. Eveline knew her husband bedded quite a few women. She knew it, but she never had to confront it because he was very discreet. He never flaunted his other women. He never embarrassed her publicly.

Justin would never get caught again. In fact, he didn't have another sexual experience until his junior year in high school. None of the girls was lining up to be with Justin back then. Maritza was an anomaly. She saw beyond his weirdness, his awkwardness. Or perhaps she was just so much of a freak that she didn't care. Her hunger for him didn't cure Justin of his shyness. He still had a problem approaching girls. He was still a bit of an outcast. Inside, however, he knew that he was special in some way to somebody. And that was enough to carry him through until his body caught up with how he felt about himself inside.

Justin now was fully caught up, sitting on this airplane to New York next to Tasha Reynolds, and he could see into his future. He could see the magazine covers, the billboard ads. It wasn't confidence, it was knowledge. He knew the things that Tasha was telling him were going to happen. And for the first time, he was excited about his life.

There was nothing exciting about heading up a rum distillery, getting married, having three kids—two boys and a girl. Maybe he'd have a few women on the side, the way his father and his father's father did. Maybe he'd enjoy the rum a little too much, the way his father did. Maybe he'd have a big house, a nice car, and all of the trappings of wealth. But there was nothing exciting about all of that for Justin.

But this excursion to New York? Now *this* was exciting.

"What's the first thing we're going to do when we land?" Justin asked Tasha.

He sounded like a kid on a long-distance trip, asking, "Are we there, yet?" Tasha thought it was endearing. It was a far cry from the stoic, almost rude young man she'd met that very first day. This was charming and it was a layer to his personality she hadn't quite expected. There was an innocence to his questioning.

"Well, first, we're going to take a limo into Manhattan to my loft," she said. "I have some business to take care of and you need to get settled. I'll show you to your room and you can unwind, watch some television, and get ready for a busy day tomorrow."

"What's going to happen tomorrow?" His eyes sparkled in anticipation of her answer.

"I have you set up for a day-long—a photo shoot," Tasha said. "We have to get your portfolio and contact sheet together so I can start sending you out on jobs. I have my best photographer meeting us at the studio first thing in the morning. So when we get back, please try to get some rest. You have to look your best."

Tasha smiled to herself as she said that. She didn't think it was possible for Justin to look anything but his best. He was absolutely perfect. The things she would have to work on with him would not be physical. But what many didn't know was that modeling was so much more than the physical. It was 90 percent attitude and confidence. Most top models are far from perfect physically—but they believe they are the hottest, the sexiest, the prettiest, the best. Even if they don't believe it, they project that image strongly enough that everyone else believes it.

While Justin certainly had an internal strength, Tasha wasn't sure if he had the attitude, that "it" thing. She would find out tomorrow. The camera doesn't lie. It would tell her all she needed to know. And if Justin didn't have "it" now, Tasha knew that by the time she was finished with him, he would. She was known for her ability to transform. Tasha Reynolds was fierce. She'd put the "it" in shit!

"What am I going to wear?" Justin had a thousand and one questions. Some of it was genuine concern. Some was nerves, from the plane ride.

As he looked out of the tiny window, he still couldn't grasp how this several-ton machine could float in the air. It was baffling and scary. The little turbulence almost made him want to vomit, but he held it together. He remembered what his mother always told him.

"Act like you've done it before," she would say. "It's never good to look like a novice. Fake it until you make it."

So he took a deep breath and tried to tune out all that was making him uncomfortable.

Why did I want to sit near the window seat?

"In some of the shots, you'll be wearing nothing," Tasha said. "But it will be a closed set. You'll be fine."

"No clothes? I don't know about that," said Justin.

His mind was certainly off the flight. Justin didn't mind posing. He had watched *Zoolander* and thought that was pretty funny. He figured he would do a few Blue Steels and call it a day. While he had no problem walking around his island without a shirt, showing *all* of his goods before a bunch of strangers was quite a different story. He wasn't comfortable at all.

"Don't tell me you're shy," said Tasha, teasingly. "You have been naked before, haven't you?"

"In the shower a few times," Justin said.

"Oh, you're funny. I knew behind that gruff exterior you had more going on. Hey, look!"

Tasha reached over Justin, pointing out of the window. The light scent of Allure tickled his nostrils.

"See, right there. The Empire State Building. If you're a good boy, I'll take you to the observation deck later on in the week. If we have time. I see I have my work cut out for me."

The Empire State Building. It looked like the souvenir his father had brought him. While it was still miles away, it stood out along the New York City skyline. It was a magnificent sight.

But many more magnificent things were about to happen to Justin Blakeman.

Chapter Six

Tasha was happy with the last few phone calls she made that night. She knew she had something big in the works with Justin. She called Jean Michel, one of the best photographers in the business. She called Anne Becker, a dynamo creative director with an impeccable eye for talent, and she called her assistant, Shera, and asked her to clear her morning.

Tasha was excited and nervous for Justin. It felt as if it was *her* first photo shoot. She wanted to make sure she got a good night's sleep, but as she leaned over to turn out her light, she paused because she heard movement. She crept downstairs to see exactly what was going on. While her houseguest seemed to be no trouble, Tasha was by instinct territorial.

"Hey, what are you still doing up?" said Tasha as she made her way to the bottom of the stairs.

"Oh, nothing. I just thought I would get a glass of water and look out the window for a while," said Justin as he walked toward the huge window just off the kitchen. "Tasha, everything is just happening so fast. I don't know what to expect. I don't even know if I *want* any of this. I feel like I'm just going along for the ride and not asking many questions and I don't think . . . no, I *know* it's not smart."

"Look, I can only imagine how you're feeling right now," said Tasha, putting her hand on his shoulder. "But let me just say that everything you are about to experience is good. I'm not going to tell you that it won't be hard at times, but I know you're about to do things other people spend a lifetime dreaming about.

"Tell you what, if for any reason you try wealth and fame and you don't like it, I give you permission to walk away."

Justin looked at her and smiled. He nodded and she headed back to bed.

"Get some sleep!" she yelled from the top of the stairs.

Justin took a sip from his glass and imagined what this wealth and fame would look like. He couldn't see it. But he trusted Tasha. And this all seemed to make her happy.

Tasha made sure that they arrived at the office at seven sharp—a half hour before anyone was expected to arrive. She told Justin to check out the wardrobe and the studio and get settled. She told him it would all be happening behind those double doors at the end of the hall.

"I'll be just down the hall in my office, checking e-mail," said Tasha.

Justin imagined heaven would look just like this: white marble floors, bone white walls, and recessed lighting. He thought Tasha's apartment was impressive, but this office, which occupied the entire forty-eighth floor overlooking Times Square, with floor-to-ceiling windows, took his breath away.

Justin couldn't help but wonder how he had gotten here. Everything was moving so quickly all around him. As soon as he was about to make sense of it all, in walked a tall, beautiful woman he assumed was a model.

"Hello, my name is Anne, and you are—?" she said in a sultry voice.

"My name is Justin," he said.

Justin could tell that she was an experienced model. She seemed to be assessing the situation and thinking rapidly as she paced the floor. She took a sketchbook out of her black Gucci sack. She did a quick survey of the studio and began to draw different poses and positioning, looking at Justin, the wardrobe, and the lighting.

She went to the wardrobe at the far end of the studio and pulled out a few items.

"Try on this and these jeans and these slacks. I want to see how they hang," said Anne.

Justin obliged without asking any questions, but he had plenty. The first: Who the fuck was this woman?

"Nah," Anne said, handing him another shirt. "I don't like that color. Try this one."

Justin went through what seemed like a hundred outfit changes before Anne settled on four outfits.

"I want to see you in the red ensemble first," she said. "Then you should change into the jeans with no shirt. Then the all-white number. And for the finale, the tuxedo. I have an idea for the tie, though. I'll be back. The shoot isn't for another hour."

Anne left the room, leaving Justin to contemplate everything that was happening.

Do I really want to do this?

That thought was turning into his mantra.

He waited around for a while and started to get impatient. He stepped outside the studio and people were bustling about. Tasha emerged from her office. She didn't want Justin roaming around the hallways. She didn't want him mingling with her staff and others. Not yet, anyway. But she decided now was as good a time as any to introduce him.

"Everybody, I'd like to introduce you to my latest discovery, Mr. Justin Blakeman," Tasha said. "He hails from Jamaica. Please make him feel at home."

It was more of a command than a request, with which almost everyone complied. Everyone was warm or cordial—except for one model who eyed Justin up and down and turned up his lip and didn't speak.

"What's his problem?" Justin said to Tasha out of the side of his mouth.

"Jealous," she said. "Escuelo was my pet project before you came along. I'm not sure if he's a keeper. He's pulling in some work, but he hasn't reached the potential that I thought he would. Part of it is his attitude. No matter what you do—whether you're a model or a plumber—a good attitude will take you so much further in life."

It was a lesson Tasha somehow knew Justin knew already. Otherwise she wouldn't have brought him to the office for his first-ever photo shoot. She couldn't wait to see if he photographed as well as he looked in real life. She knew that the lens of the camera would cut through and capture his true essence as a person.

Tasha had three photo studios inside her agency. She'd known when she built her company that she didn't want to be dependent on anyone—and having to lease space at the rates they charged in the city would be cost prohibitive. She was savvy enough to have her own space so that record labels, magazines, and other smaller modeling agencies could rent it for the day.

Anne came back about thirty minutes before the shoot with a few ties she'd pulled from her own closet. One was very colorful and the other was a simple black string tie. She told Justin she had the idea of having his tuxedo shirt open, with the string tie just hanging loose. Justin liked that. He was starting to like Anne, too.

Tasha, Justin, and Anne made their way to the main studio to discuss the layout for the shoot. The photographer, Jean Michel, arrived shortly after. He was a personal friend of Tasha and one of the best in the business—Tasha surrounded herself with only the best in the business. He'd been there from the beginning of her agency and had helped shape it into the Reynolds Agency. Jean Michel did all of the portfolios and was one of the few people Tasha trusted. He could predict a winner on sight. Together with Anne, there was no way Justin was going to fail.

"So, Miss Tasha, where did you find this one?" said Jean Michel.

"Jamaica," she said. "Isn't he beautiful?"

Justin couldn't believe they were talking about him as if he wasn't even standing there. He was about to say something, but then he decided to just watch and listen.

"We'll see." Jean Michel winked at Justin. "We'll see what the camera says. Take your shirt off."

"Gee, you don't waste any time, do you?" Justin said, unbuttoning his shirt.

"Wait a minute," Tasha said. "I want to go over a few things with Justin first. Give us about fifteen minutes."

"Okay. But you know my time is valuable. Since I'm not charging you the regular rate, the least you could do is be respectful of my time," Jean Michel said.

"Don't start with that diva stuff, Jean," said Tasha, wagging a playful finger at him. "Fifteen minutes. I promise. Love you!"

He walked out of the studio.

Tasha had to give Justin a crash course in Modeling 101. She had created several models. Even when she was at Wilhelmina, her forte was discovering and cultivating talent. This one was going to be easy. Not like some of the others. Most of the would-be models that Tasha came across had preconceived notions of how to walk, how to pose. They were vain and conceited, cocky, and absolutely insecure.

It was Justin's assuredness, his complete lack of ego that was so appealing to Tasha. He had no idea how beautiful he was, and more important, he didn't seem to care. He wasn't concerned at all with "products," and what he would use on his hair or skin. He didn't wax his eyebrows, or any other part of his body. He had very little hair, and what he had didn't seem to bother him. It didn't bother Tasha, either. It was manly—that thatch of hair leading from his chest to his private regions. It seemed naturally well groomed. Justin was a man, a BVD-wearing, regular-soap-using, wash-and-wear-and-be-out-of-the-house-in-five-minutes sort of dude. And Tasha loved it.

It was as if Tasha had a huge lump of clay and she could mold it into the exact model she wanted Justin to be.

"I have a vision for you to become the most famous male model ever," she said. "Yours will be a household face.

"Now when you're in front of the camera, pretend that the camera is a beautiful woman," Tasha said. "Think about what you feel when you see a beautiful woman. Imagine that the camera is someone you would love to meet. If you allow yourself to feel all of that, the camera will pick it up."

"I think I can do that," Justin said.

"I think so, too," Tasha said. "The key to this is *not* to pose. You don't want to *look* like you're modeling. You want the camera to look into your soul. When you look at the spread of a really good model, it's as if you can see exactly what's on their minds and in their hearts, what they're feeling in that moment. They are able to convey so much with just their eyes or how they hold their mouths."

Tasha handed Justin a few portfolios of some of the top models in the agency.

"Flip through these quickly and see what I'm talking about," Tasha said.

Justin started flipping through the pages.

"I want you to be a student of this game," Tasha said. "This is a business. It's not enough for you just to look good. You have to understand that what makes someone successful isn't just how they look.

"Cindy Crawford, a beautiful woman with a giant raisin on

her face. Kate Moss, quite common and in some circles unattractive. Alek Wek. Need I say more? They carry themselves with a certain knowing. They *know* they are something special, and because of that, so does the world.

"So where do you see yourself in five years?" Tasha asked Justin the question she asked all of her new models. She needed to know if they were on the same page and if they actually saw themselves as being as successful as she did.

"With you," he said matter-of-factly.

The response caught Tasha off guard. So she decided to ignore the comment and chalk it up to his playful nature.

"Seriously, do you see the billboards, the television commercials, the money pouring in?" Tasha prodded. "You have to see it for it to happen."

"You know, I took this journey with you because I wanted to see a lot of things I have never seen, experience a lot of things I have never experienced," Justin said. "I'd rather not look into the crystal ball and try to map out my future. I just want to live right now and enjoy every minute of it. I'll leave all of that vision stuff up to you. So what do you want me to do when that photographer comes back in here? I want to be perfect."

You already are, Tasha thought.

He *had* mastered the perfect walk. Now he mastered the perfect pose. He was so relaxed and carefree in front of the camera that Tasha didn't have to remind him to "look natural," or coach him about making faces as she'd had to with others before him.

Jean Michel seemed to love working with Justin—especially the naked shot.

Tasha had never seen Jean Michel actually react to seeing anyone naked. He was a real pro, nothing fazed him, but Tasha caught him pausing when Justin removed his last item of clothing. She caught Jean Michel taking a deep breath. It was a subtle reaction, but it spoke volumes.

Yes, indeed. This Justin was *quite* a find.

Chapter Seven

It was their third game of backgammon and they had each won a game.

"Whoever wins this one gets whatever they want," Justin said to Tasha.

And so the teasing began—again.

It was a dance that had been going on for weeks now. It was there when they would brush against each other in the morning in the kitchen. It was there when Justin was on a photo shoot and Tasha, who was rarely at any of her models' shoots, would be there, fixing his shirt or smoothing out his pants, making sure he looked perfect.

Justin had moved from Tasha's pet project to Tasha's obsession. And it was becoming increasingly more difficult to deny. Tasha knew her own rules and she had been playing by them pretty hard, until now.

"Whatever they want? I don't know about that!" she said.

"What! Are you nervous about what I might want?" Justin continued to toy with her.

"Oh, hell no. I'm not losing!" Tasha said, playfully upset. "I'm worried about what *I* might want."

Tasha looked at him and suddenly realized how lonely her life had become. She had been so consumed with work, with building her empire, that she hadn't had time to enjoy the company of a man. Since . . . well, she'd had a few sexual encounters with Renaldo—her "fuck buddy," as Jean Michel referred to him. But that was basically just to scratch an itch. Renaldo was always willing, and grateful, to come over in the middle of the night, no words exchanged, strip down to nothing, and let Tasha have her way—which was usually her on top, screwing him fast and hard.

There was very little foreplay—actually there was very little play at all. Renaldo came over to handle Tasha's business. And he always satisfied. When he was done, he knew to leave as quietly and effortlessly as he'd arrived. Tasha didn't really enjoy his company—just his dick.

But Justin was something else. When she'd spotted him that day on that Jamaican road, she'd known he was special, but never in her wildest imagination did she think she would fall for him.

Tasha "Ice Queen" Reynolds was actually melting.

Love? Oh, no! Tasha didn't *do* love. But it was something. It was love-*ish*.

She loved the way he made his eggs. She loved the way he brushed his teeth, the way he shaved. She loved the casual way he carried around his sexiness, just tossing it about aimlessly as if it was an old sweater—not flaunting it or trying too hard, just being sexy. Tasha could talk to Justin about anything and he was a very good listener. He wouldn't offer advice unless she asked for it, and when he did, it was always simple and right on target. He was great to watch movies with—even chick flicks. And he actually could play chess, and Scrabble—Tasha's favorite game. It was hard finding someone who could challenge her, but Justin seemed to have an answer for every one of Tasha's questions.

He's too fucking perfect, she thought. *Nobody's this damn perfect!*

"The only way you will win this game is if I *let* you win," Justin said, jarring Tasha out of her thoughts about him. "And I just might do that. I want to know what it is you want so much that you're scared to actually declare it."

Tasha knew she was in some dangerous waters. She knew this was perhaps one moment she should back away from, but couldn't. She really did like Justin. Tasha more than liked him, she needed him. She would never admit it to a soul, not even herself, but she needed him to be home when she got there. She needed him there when she awakened. It made her feel safe—safer than she had ever felt in her life. She got to breathe around Justin. And for once, she could let down her weave and be herself—or, more important, with him, she was finding out who that self was.

The person Tasha had become was someone she didn't quite like very much. But that bitch was essential. She had made it possible not only to launch the agency, but also to put the entire industry on notice. But now the persona had become the person. And Tasha looked at Justin and realized she didn't have a single friend.

There was no one in her life with whom she could discuss her dreams or her fears—or her feelings for him. She was in her own world, marching to her own beat, and very much alone.

Justin, with his youthful innocence, his foreign naiveté, and his laid-back, soft-spoken demeanor, had somehow made it easy for Tasha to open up.

One night Tasha came home from a particularly tough day. One of her top models was flaking on her and threatening to leave for another agency. She had not had one mutiny since she started, but it was inevitable. Models, as a breed, aren't the most loyal or reasonable. Many are prima donnas who need a lot of hand-holding, ego stroking, and babying. Tasha wasn't the babying type. So she would have her battles and they would all go her way—until this time.

"Fucking diva bullshit!" she said, to no one in particular, whipping her hat off and throwing it on the table by the door. "I *made* that bitch!"

Tasha never cursed in public and she rarely cursed in private, but this time she was pissed.

Justin came from his room with a concerned look on his face. He didn't open his mouth. He didn't say, "What's the matter?" He figured she would tell him eventually. His presence, though, was enough. It was like a truth serum and it all came pouring out.

"Now that Mira has a multimillion-dollar contract with Revlon, she thinks she doesn't need me!" Tasha continued. "She said, 'Why am I paying you all of this commission? You need to take less.' Less?! Does she think she *woke up* being one of the top faces in the world? When I found her skinny behind in the Bronx, wearing those tight-ass jeans, those Airforce Ones, and that ugly perm, did she really believe she would be a Revlon girl? I mean, *really*?!"

Tasha could barely catch her breath as she was fueling her own anger. But then she looked at Justin and his light brown eyes just sucked her in, calming her instantly.

"Can you believe that shit?!" she said. "What do you think?"

"Let her go," Justin said.

"Are you crazy?! She is a cash-fucking-cow! I'm not going to just walk away from what I built, what I worked for! She can't just leave me."

"I believe people should want to be where they are, and if they aren't happy, you should let them go," Justin said. "What is that saying about letting a bird go?"

"Yeah, yeah. If it stays gone it was never yours . . ."

" . . . but if it comes back . . ." Justin paused. "She *will* come back. Actually, I believe she will never leave—if you calmly call her into a meeting, and you look at her, without any anger or venom, and you say, 'Mira, I want to thank you for being a part of creating this dream. I have enjoyed all that you have accomplished while being here. You have contributed greatly. I am sorry you won't be here for what's coming next. But I wish you well. You're free to go.' If you do that, she will think about everything you did for her and she will realize that there will be something more to come that she will be missing out on. No one wants to miss out on something great. And more important, no one wants to be just let go—especially not someone like Mira."

Justin was right. Mira was more than a handful. She needed to be the center of everyone's universe. She needed to have all activity revolve around her. The first day Justin had met her, she'd treated him like the water boy, someone to go fetch her things. And he quietly and politely got her everything she wanted. And when he brought her the final item—a comb from the makeup room—he held her hand and said, "You will be a fine person one day."

It was a disarming tactic Justin had learned from his ma-ma. Mira was quite puzzled. She didn't know whether it was a compliment—which she was used to—or an insult, which it absolutely was. She decided it was a compliment, smiled, and thanked him. But it troubled her. His words stuck with her and she treated him with respect after that.

Justin had that way about him. That's what I'm growing to lo—she started to think—like about him. She decided to follow his advice about Mira. She somehow knew that it would work.

She also knew she would win this game of backgammon. Then she would do what she had been dying to do for weeks.

As it turned out, Justin didn't have to let her win. She won outright, rolling a string of double sixes that was unnatural. She beat him handily. And as she put her last round white piece into the receptacle, and Justin feigned disgust over the loss, she reached over with her free hand and grabbed the back of his head, pulling him to her.

Justin was startled. Before he could get the, "What—," as in "What are you doing?" out of his mouth, Tasha had her mouth over his.

She wanted to devour every inch of Justin's juicy, thick lips. She nibbled his bottom lip like it was a ripe strawberry, one she didn't want to break for fear that the juice would run all over.

Justin's surprise was replaced quickly by arousal.

He pushed the backgammon game out of the way, pieces flying everywhere, as he grabbed Tasha and lifted her to the couch. They'd been playing on pillows on the high-gloss, hardwood floors.

But the oversize chenille couch would be more comfortable for what Justin was about to get into.

Tasha tried to take control of the situation, the way she did everything, but she had awakened a sleeping bear in Justin. With one hand, he pinned both of her arms over her head as he used his other hand to undo her pants and take them off. His arm span allowed him to do it pretty easily, but Tasha pretended to protest by wiggling back and forth.

"Be still," Justin said, in the richest baritone. Tasha, almost hypnotized, complied.

Justin let go and slowed down the pace. He undid every button on her shirt, as slowly as he could, watching her try not to squirm. The heat between Tasha's legs was about to set what was left of her pubic hair, after a Brazilian waxing, on fire. She wanted to mount Justin. She wanted to ride him. She had no idea what she was in for.

Tasha lay there, her trim belly exposed and her red lace bra ready to pop. It was a front clasp and Justin used his thumb and pointer finger to release Tasha's ample C-cup-size breasts. Her nipples looked like the nipples on a Playtex bottle—perfect, thick, and big.

Justin swooped down on her left nipple, swirling his tongue around it as if he was eating a tiny ice-cream cone. Then he gave the right one equal attention. Tasha just closed her eyes and moaned.

"Don't move," Justin whispered in her ear before making his way down her body. That command was an impossibility. Tasha tried to reach for Justin's zipper. Why were his pants still on? she wondered. The bulge looked as if it would rip the seam of his jeans.

But Justin grabbed her hand again. He was fully dressed. He didn't intend on taking off his clothes until he was done with the appetizer.

Justin traced a path with his tongue, from her nipples down to the center of her stomach. Tasha's chest heaved; she couldn't catch her breath when he settled for a few seconds on her navel. That was one of her spots that few of her lovers knew about. He had found it instinctually. It was like a jolt of electricity being released on her clit as he gently worked his tongue in and around her belly button, which was a twinny, a cross between an inny and an outie.

He then traced her bulging clit, which was practically sticking out from her silk Victoria's Secrets. They were already damp from Tasha's juices, but Justin made them pour, sucking slowly and gently from the outside of her panties until Tasha was practically screaming, "Fuck me!"

"Shhh," he said. "I got this."

He pulled down her panties, releasing a heat he had never felt before. He plunged in with his long, thick tongue, right into the middle of the creamiest pussy he had ever tasted. His first girlfriend had taught him the art of eating a woman, and Justin had been a very good student. Tasha had had many experiences in her life, but this was the best sexual experience she had ever had.

She came three times before Justin even took his clothes off.

She didn't think she could come again. Each orgasm was increasingly more violent. The last one came while Justin was pinching her nipples gently as he quickly poked and nipped her clit with his tongue and lips. Those lips. They were the softest, moistest, most succulent lips Tasha had ever felt, and to have them on her clit was indescribable. Justin knew exactly what he was doing.

While she was recovering from orgasm number three, he took his time getting undressed.

Tasha had seen the man practically naked before. But actually seeing him naked was a sight she hadn't quite prepared for. Her stomach dropped when she saw his perfect erection, nine and a half inches of rich, dark, thick perfection. She reached out to touch it. She had to touch it. She could barely close her hand around it, it was so thick. Justin moaned as a droplet formed on the tip. Tasha licked her lips. She had to taste him—had to! She didn't know what she wanted more—him inside her mouth or him inside her.

She satisfied her oral fixation first. She licked from just under the tip, catching all the juice that was leaking. She tried to take his entire dick into her mouth, swirling her tongue on the underside as she came up for air.

Tasha had Justin where she wanted him, on his back, as she went to work on his member, which seemed to swell another inch, if that was possible. The veins in his dick were pulsating; she could feel the fluid rushing through them with every suck, with every lick. It was driving her crazy. She wanted to mount him badly. But before she could, he flipped her over. It was a smooth, martial-arts-like move. Tasha had no idea how she'd ended up on her stomach. She *never* ended up on her stomach!

Justin reached under, lifting her belly so that her perfect ass was in the air, and he mounted her from the back. He tapped slowly at her pussy door, wetting the head of his dick with her juices. He then put just the head in, and he could feel her walls closing in, squeezing.

Tasha had some tricks of her own. She pushed her ass hard against him. He was playing with her and Tasha didn't want to play. She wanted to fuck.

With her one thrust against him, she had completely filled up with him. Justin gasped. He didn't expect it to be so hot and so tight. He could barely get off ten pumps before he shot so hard into her that Tasha swore she could feel it in her chest.

She had come again on stroke seven. Tasha was through. Like Roberto Durán in his fight against Sugar Ray, she wanted *no más*. She couldn't handle anymore. Tasha knew if she came one more time that way, she might need to be committed because she would lose her mind.

"Oh shit!" Tasha managed to say between breaths. "*No más!*" They both smiled.

Justin lay there, already getting hard again. But he knew she wasn't ready for round two. There would be time for that. He wanted to just lie there, holding her still trembling body, saying not a word.

He wanted to enjoy this moment.

In his mind's eye

My first girlfriend was a whore. She slept with just about every guy in our school and I liked that about her. She was experienced and she knew exactly what she wanted and how she wanted it.

Natalie was five feet four, with dark chocolate skin and long, silky, curly hair. She was very petite and had the most beautiful, perky set of breasts I had ever seen. Actually, they were the first pair of breasts I had ever seen in person—outside of my mother's, which was by accident (and that certainly didn't count).

We were both sixteen. We hooked up while working together in biology class, of all things. Natalie told me I had nice lips. Nice lips? Me? The first thing I was ever teased about were my lips. I was called everything from "liver lips" to "mush mouth" to "Sir Lips." I was extremely self-conscious about the size of my lips, to the point where I would try to hide them. I would keep my lips tucked in and, as a result, didn't talk much. When Natalie, one of the prettiest girls in the school, told me she thought I had nice lips, she had me.

She must have looked forward to the challenge of teaching me how to use those lips. Our first kiss was in a park we cut through as I was walking her home. We leaned on a tree, and she grabbed my face and pulled me close. I didn't know what I was doing. But shortly after I started kissing her, she pulled back, wiping her mouth with the back of her hand.

"Whoa, whoa, killer!" she said. "You have to slow down. And all of that spit. Uh-uh! That simply will not do."

I was so nervous and so eager, I just moved in at a hundred miles an hour, mouth open, tongue ready. I had seen people kiss on television and in a few R-rated movies and I thought I had it down. Natalie was the best teacher I could have asked for. By the time she was done with me, I not only was a very good kisser, I was also an expert at performing cunnilingus. I had to look that one up when she told me she wanted me to do it to her.

I got so good at it that she said she was ruined. She couldn't see herself being with anyone else. I had her whipped. I had the school whore whipped. But by the end of the summer, I was over Natalie. I had confidence, had put on about twenty-five pounds, had grown another two inches, and was getting quite a bit of attention.

I wanted to see if I really had it. I needed to know if I could have that same touch with someone other than Natalie.

I went after Pamela. She was shy, sweet, and cute. Every boy in school had tried, but none had gotten very far at all.

Chapter Eight

Tasha took the pancake mix out of the cabinet. Every Saturday, after a week of starving herself, Tasha looked forward to some pancakes. If there were some fresh blueberries or strawberries available, she would throw those in, too. Still conscientious about her health, she would make the pancakes with whole wheat flour, an egg substitute, and soy milk. Even in her indulgences, Tasha had to be responsible and sensible and completely in control.

Control was what kept Tasha together. She needed it. She demanded it. She even had a team come in twice a week to make sure that everything in her home was dusted and cleaned and in order.

But for the first time in her life, she was doing something completely out of character—completely out of control. While others in her industry experimented with cocaine—hell, some were out-and-out addicts—Tasha always passed. She could never imagine snorting or injecting something into her body.

She'd once attended a party at a well-known model's home where there was a room designated for getting high. It was set up with stations. One station had a Tiffany silver platter, piled high with cocaine. It was surrounded by small, attractive mirrors and razor blades for those who wanted to snort. There was a Waterford drinking glass filled with sterile needles on a table, with baking soda, tiny silver spoons, bottles of Evian, and a gold-plated lighter for those who wanted to shoot up. There were glass pipes and perfectly formed cocaine rocks for those who wanted to smoke. There were private, VIP-only areas where people could go and do what they wanted to do, if they didn't want company.

And with the drugs came the sex. In the modeling industry—as with most of the entertainment business—there was very little sexual inhibition. Women had sex with women and didn't consider it lesbian behavior. It was just sex. Men had sex with men and no one batted an eyelash. It was just sex. Tasha was a bit of a prude. She'd never had a one-night stand in her life. She thought that was reserved for people who were nasty and lacked self-control and dignity. She had her "fuck-buddies" over for a booty call, but those were *always* men she knew.

Tasha was grateful that she was never driven by sex. It wasn't high on her list of things to do. Sex didn't really excite Tasha. She got off more on seeing one of her models make it to Hollywood. She damn near had an orgasm the first time she saw Tek on a billboard in Times Square for Calvin Klein. She almost had multiple orgasms when she opened her business and in the process stole two of Ford's top models.

But nothing, absolutely nothing, compared to the night she'd had with Justin. It was the first time in her life that Tasha was consumed with something other than fashion and business and ruling the modeling world. She couldn't wait to make these pancakes, take them into the bedroom, and feed him. She also couldn't wait to smear his body with syrup and have her dessert.

Tasha wanted to continue what had been started the night before. Just thinking about it, as she poured five perfect pancakes onto the griddle in the center of her restaurant-quality Viking stove, made her coochie twitch.

Justin was on his way to the stardom she'd promised. He had a few runway assignments and a couple of magazine spreads. And Tasha had just gotten a call to book him for British *Vogue*. He was well on his way.

But she was starting to realize there was a part of her that didn't want to share him with the world. She was starting to realize that she wanted him all to herself, all *for* herself.

Chapter Nine

Anne delivered Justin's portfolio personally. She wanted to surprise Tasha. Anne had worked very hard on selecting the right shots and putting it all together, and she had determined that it was a masterpiece, one of the best she had ever done.

It was still in the box, with its elaborate wrapping, from the printer when she arrived at Tasha's agency, walked past her assistant, and right into her office. Tasha was on a call, and when she looked up and saw Anne, she hurried to get off.

"What's that?" Tasha said.

Anne just smiled, and Tasha knew. Her insides jumped. Tasha felt like a seven-year-old on Christmas morning who still believed in Santa Claus.

"Come, come, come!" she squealed, out of character. "Let me see!"

"Okay! Okay!" Anne said. "It's just a portfolio. Geez!"

Tasha opened the box and started immediately flipping through the pages. She seemed to be in a trance as she drank in each image.

"He's a special one, isn't he?" Anne said.

"Uh-huh," Tasha grunted, not looking up.

Anne noticed something in Tasha that she hadn't seen before. The two had known each other for more than five years. While Tasha rarely opened up to anyone—she kept a cool facade and had a standoffish demeanor—Anne had been able to chip through some of Tasha's front and become her friend. It was a friendship that developed naturally, mainly because Anne was so strong. She wasn't threatened or intimidated by Tasha the way most were. The two had a lot in common. Anne was just as successful. And she had a similar I-don't-give-a-fuck attitude.

There was something mysterious about Anne that Tasha found intriguing. Anne was not a typical woman. Despite her beauty—and she was quite a looker—she chose not to use her looks. In fact, she downplayed them, often dressing in loose-fitting clothes and covering her mane with assorted hats.

But what Tasha loved most about Anne was the no-nonsense way she expressed herself. Anne didn't mince words.

"You have crossed the line, missy!" Anne said in the sternest voice she could muster up.

"What are you talking about?" said a surprised Tasha, who finally looked up from Justin's portfolio.

"You're fucking him," Anne said matter-of-factly.

"You're tripping!" Tasha said. But she couldn't stop blushing.

"Am I?" said Anne, not letting her eyes leave Tasha's.

The staring contest lasted a minute before Tasha burst out laughing. Anne still didn't crack a smile.

"You know that's a no-no!" Anne said. "You cannot run a business like this by getting caught up in your models. It will *ruin* you."

"You're going to have to trust me on this one," Tasha said. "I know what I'm doing. I have this one under control."

"You can *never* have a man under control!" Anne said. "Temporarily, perhaps. But not completely and certainly not forever. Come on, Tasha. I thought you were smarter than this!"

Tasha felt defensive and was starting to get angry. Anne needed to mind her own business, she thought. But she didn't want to start a fight with her. She needed Anne. More important, she respected Anne. She was the only friend Tasha had. She didn't have any childhood friends, and since coming to New York she'd been so driven she hadn't wanted to foster any close relationships.

With the cattiness of the fashion business, it was difficult to find a friend—especially a woman. There just weren't a whole lot of people Tasha could trust. They either wanted to see her fail or they wanted to be her. Anne was real, honest, raw, and totally secure—which was disarming to most, but completely welcome to Tasha.

"Anne, you're overstepping a bit," Tasha said.

"No, *you're* overstepping with *him,*" Anne said calmly. "Tell me what happens when Mr. Jamaica blows up and starts making a bunch of money and has every kind of ass he never imagined thrown at him. How is that going to have an impact on your business? Are you going to be able to see him successful even if he's not *with* you?"

"Justin's not like that . . ."

"They never are, in the beginning," Anne said. "But, Tasha, you've been around long enough to know that things more often than not change. And when feelings are involved it can get ugly. I just don't want to ever see you get ugly."

Anne touched Tasha's cheek tenderly, which lightened the mood a bit.

"You're far too beautiful for that," Anne said. "I loved watching you build all of this over the years. I knew you were going to be something when you were with Wilhelmina. I know you will be the queen of all of this one day. So please forgive me for not wanting to see you blow it all because of some man."

"I know, Annie," Tasha said. "But he's not just some man. He is really different. You need to get to know him. I have never met anyone like him."

"So it's love?"

"Well, don't go too far," Tasha said. "I'm not crazy. But I'm really feeling him—and it feels *good*. I haven't had a man of my own since . . . I can't remember when. He's easy. He's not in the way. And I will never let him get in the way. If I see it getting crazy, I will pull back."

"Promise?"

"Promise," Tasha said, squeezing Anne's hand reassuringly. "I want everything you see for me and more. I'm not slipping. But you have to promise to help me make this guy a star."

"Okay," Anne said. "But be careful what you ask for."

Chapter Ten

Tasha Reynolds allowed herself one indulgence as she sat at her glass desk in her corner office on the forty-eighth floor of 1545 Broadway. Every day, she gave herself fifteen minutes to admire the view she had worked so hard to acquire.

The floor-to-ceiling windows gave her an almost panoramic view of the greatness of New York City: Times Square, with its giant Discover card sign that had replaced the giant Nissin Cup Noodles, the megasize poster of Puffy with his fist punched in the air à la John Carlos at the 1968 Olympics, the Naked Cowboy, and the news ticker that wrapped around the building housing the ABC studios were directly in front of her.

To the east side she could see the top of the Empire State

Building, which was lit at the top in red, white, and blue. To the north, she could see Central Park, which looked like a beautiful, untouched forest from where she sat. From Tasha's window, she could see the best of everything New York City had to offer. Because of her place in life, she got to enjoy New York—really enjoy it—the way few could. She got to dine at the best restaurants, got to sit at the best tables with the best service. She was driven everywhere, so the traffic that plagued many commuters never fazed Tasha, who could conduct business from the back of a Lincoln Town Car during the week or from her Suburban when she felt like a change of pace. When she did drive, it was in a Mercedes SL500 convertible in the summer and her Mercedes SUV in the winter—and never during rush hour. For Tasha, New York was exactly what she had imagined it would be when she daydreamed in Augusta, Georgia, about making it big there.

She *was* big.

And for fifteen minutes a day, Tasha allowed herself to really enjoy that feeling. She reflected on how high she had climbed. She took this time to appreciate what her hard work had allowed: not just this office, but industry fame and more money than she'd ever imagined having, coming from that town in Georgia known more for its golf courses than anything else—until now.

Country folk just didn't get to do all of this. Most of her cousins and other relatives worked at low-paying factory jobs, which were dwindling. Others worked at Piggly Wiggly or the local Wal-Mart. And there was one cousin who was a dispatcher in the sheriff's department. But Tasha was the only Reynolds who had officially made it outside of Augusta.

Tonight she was going to take a little more than fifteen minutes. This was a special night. It was New Year's Eve—a night when she would reflect on not just the year that had passed but on the year that was to come.

For the last three years, Tasha had held a little New Year's Eve bash in her office. She invited over a few friends and clients, kept the lights really low, had food catered, and watched the ball drop as they toasted in the new year with endless bottles of Veuve Clicquot and Dom Pérignon. They had the complete experience of the millions who crammed into the area below her window, minus the frigid temperatures, the possibility of being crushed in the crowd, and being herded like cattle through the barricades the police put up for protection.

This new year was going to be the best ever because she had the perfect man to enjoy it with. It was the one thing that had eluded her up to this point. Tasha was able to get absolutely everything else she wanted. She demanded it. But she could never seem to find that special one.

When she was a teenager, she'd imagined she would grow up and be Taimak's wife. He was so fine in *The Last Dragon*. She had daydreamed about him, writing "Taimak loves Tasha" on her notebook, hearts all around their names. They would be the perfect TNT, dynamite together. He was sensitive, yet strong. His body was absolutely perfect. Tasha's first masturbation fantasy was about making love to Taimak in the rain in a park near her home, the rainwater dripping down his body. If she concentrated, she could taste the mix of sweat and fresh rainwater.

Then she went through her phase of being attracted to thugs.

She met Nashim on her way home one evening, in her convertible. It was a hot summer night and he was walking from somewhere with his shirt off. Yes, Tasha was a sucker for a nice body. His tight, mocha skin glistened under the streetlights. She stared at him while she waited for the light to change. She never imagined that they would ever talk. But before her light turned green, he had walked over to her car.

"What's up, sugar," he said, in the deepest voice she'd heard outside of Isaac Hayes's. "Where're you headed?"

To her place. Tasha had never picked up a man in her life—let alone picked one up off the street. But the connection was instant, and before she knew it, Mr. Beefcake had Miss Tasha's legs in the air and it was on. Nashim was more than a one-night stand—he lasted a couple of weeks. The sex was that good. But it was never going to be much else. It wasn't as if she could be seen in public with him at events. He couldn't be the man sitting next to her in Bryant Park during Fashion Week.

Tasha convinced herself she didn't have time for a real relationship. That would only get in her way. She didn't need a man asking her, "When are you coming home?" and "Where are you going tonight?" and "What's for dinner?" She didn't want to have to answer to anyone, appease anyone, or please anyone—unless it was her pleasure, too. She was on a mission and that mission didn't include a man.

And then along came Justin—not asking for anything, not wanting anything, just being there, giving Tasha everything she didn't think she needed.

She could hear the crowd mingling outside her door. She could even hear Justin's distinctive laugh. He must be entertaining the people. He really knew how to make everyone feel at ease.

• • •

The party was everything Justin had imagined.

Justin had vowed that he would be in Times Square for the dropping of the ball way back when he was in Jamaica, before he had ever thought about actually getting on a plane and being in New York. He just knew that one day he would be there. He never imagined, however, that he would be there like this—standing on top of it all like some sort of Greek god, looking over the masses of people below.

He could see it all from the huge reception area of the Reynolds Agency. There were about fifty people in the room—models and their friends, colleagues, and a few clients. But to Justin, he was part of the millions below.

Tasha finally emerged from her office—dressed in a pair of black palazzo pants and a matching black halter top. She looked fabulous. She had her hair up with a few curls cascading down in the front.

She took a glass from one of the waiters carrying a tray of champagne and tapped on the side of it with an hors d'oeuvres fork.

"Everyone, may I have your attention, please," Tasha began, and the crowd settled down to near silence. "I want to say that this has been an incredible year! We have seen more success than I could possibly have imagined. And it is because of your hard work and energy. I just want to thank each and every one of you for helping me realize a dream that I had so many years ago. I want to thank you all for being a part of this. And I want you to know that we are not satisfied. Next year will be even greater. Cheers. To you!"

Everyone raised their glasses, a few clinked with one another, a few hugged and kissed. Tasha sought out Justin and gave him a nod and a smile. They were still not public with their relationship, and he knew there would be special time for them later on when no one else was around. He was content with that. He was proud within himself, looking at this queen preside over her court with such command.

He smiled back and winked. The look said it all to Tasha.

Chapter Eleven

Tasha handed Justin his first-class ticket to London. He was getting used to the first-class star treatment. British *Vogue* had selected him and another Reynolds model, Dorian, for a provocative spread. There wasn't much information about it other than that it would be hot and would pull in fifty thousand dollars apiece for the pair, with all expenses paid.

"Are you sure you don't want to go with us?" Justin pleaded.

"Of course I want to go," Tasha said. "I haven't been to London in over a year. It would be great to go there with you, show you the sights, enjoy the food and the nightlife. But in case you haven't noticed, I have a company to run. I have a deadline to meet. It's a crazy time right now, Justin. But you're in good hands. Dorian will take care of you."

Justin didn't really know Dorian. They had seen each other in passing, around the office and at the New Year's Eve party, but Justin hadn't warmed to him.

"Good hands? With the tin man? Come on, he's so stiff. And white," Justin said. "Does he even like black people?"

"Oh, yes, he loves black people," Tasha said with a knowing smile. Dorian especially loved black *men.* "There's more to him than you can see. Just relax and try to have some fun. More important, the man is a pure pro. Watch him closely and you will learn a lot. In front of the camera, Dorian is far from stiff. He's fierce."

Tasha had put Justin through extensive training to get him ready for the grueling business. He was doing well, but there were some nuances that he could definitely pick up. This trip to London, alone, might push Justin to another level.

"It will be good for you to be there without someone holding your hand," she said. "You're a big boy."

Justin came up behind her, wrapping his arms around her waist, pressing his groin into her behind.

"I'm a really big boy," he said teasingly. "But you know that already."

"Boy, you better be careful before I take you into that bathroom and handle you," Tasha warned him. "Now why are you trying to get me all heated when you have a plane to catch in less than two hours?"

"I want you to miss me," he said. "I want you to think about me constantly while I'm gone."

Justin nuzzled his nose into the nape of Tasha's neck as she closed her eyes. The tingly sensation of having him so close to her was almost too much for her to contain herself. They had made love before coming to the office, but she had a seemingly insatiable appetite for Justin. While the two of them never talked about their relationship and what it was exactly, there was an understanding.

Tasha wanted to sit him down and tell him that she never slept with her models and that they shouldn't act like lovers around anyone else—especially while at the agency. She wanted to lecture him about public displays of affection. She wanted to script his every move. But she kind of liked being Justin's woman. She liked belonging to this man. And she didn't want to ruin how it felt for her.

Somehow, Justin understood everything without Tasha telling him. He never acted like her boyfriend in front of anyone. He was her creation, and that's how it appeared to anyone who was looking. She was the Zen master; he was the good student.

Justin didn't say much to Dorian, other than hello, during the nearly nine-hour flight. He was lost in his thoughts and lost in his music. He had downloaded more than three thousand songs—more than enough music to take him to Africa and back, if he needed. He had a Tasha playlist that kicked off with Robin Thicke's "Lost Without You," and he let Tamia's "Can't Get Enough" and "Last First Kiss" carry him over the Atlantic. There was one sexy Maxwell hit after the next, a few Lionel Richie classics, something by India.Arie and Justin Timberlake, and, of course, John Legend.

Dorian seemed content to catch up on some reading. He was ripping through *The Secret* and he had the latest installment of *The Ritz Harper Chronicles* for when he tired of the self-help, motivational vibe and wanted a little juicy junk reading.

The two couldn't have been more polar opposite—which was exactly why they were chosen: Justin was new, fresh faced, wide eyed, black, and rough around the edges, and Dorian was the rising superstar, the next Marcus Schenkenberg. He had the same dirty blond good looks, the pouty mouth, and those searing eyes. In Europe, white was the rave, and Dorian was as white as they came—skin of smooth alabaster, a body chiseled out of the finest porcelain.

The concept for the shoot was a human bowl of vanilla ice cream with chocolate fudge poured on top. Justin was the chocolate fudge.

When they landed, there was a car waiting to take them directly to the shoot. There was no time for dropping off bags and unwinding. They hit the ground and went right to work. The two spent five hours in various provocative poses, mostly half naked. They wore skin-toned thongs.

Justin was not only nervous, he was very uncomfortable. As he was listening to the photographer's vision for the shoot, he began to fidget and pace. He had never in his life been this close physically to another man—not on purpose. The photographer wanted a few shots with Justin lying on top of Dorian, front to front.

"I ain't no fucking batty boy," Justin growled under his breath. While he rarely showed any emotion—let alone anger—this was really messing with his sensibilities.

"Don't worry," Dorian assured him playfully. "I have no desire to fuck you. I don't even find you attractive."

"Yeah, right!" Justin said, trying not to laugh, but he couldn't help it. The ice was broken. Justin, still reluctant, relaxed a bit. They also had some beer and wine on the set. By the end of the shoot, the two were so relaxed that Justin didn't notice how comfortable he had really become.

"Okay, Dorian, turn your head a bit to the left!" the photographer said, barking out another order. "And you, Justin, I need you to move into him, just a little bit closer. Okay, now, closer . . . closer . . ."

Justin was inches from Dorian's face.

"Hold it. Hold it!" the photographer said. "Good! Great! That's perfect. You guys are pros. Just a little longer . . ."

Justin was holding his breath. He was close enough to smell the traces of the black bean soup Dorian had had for lunch and that had settled on his top lip. Justin could feel Dorian's breaths coming through his nostrils, blowing gently on Justin's cheek. Maybe it was the time, maybe it was the way Dorian had about him that put Justin at ease, maybe it was the wine, but Justin was finally okay.

With everything.

"Hold it!" the photographer snapped. "And . . . it's a wrap. You guys were terrific. I got some *really* great shots!"

Compliments were hard to come by in this business. You were just expected to get it right. Most models are paid well enough to never need a compliment. So it must have been a great shoot, Justin thought. The two men went back to the changing room to get dressed.

Dorian stepped out of his thong and slipped into a pair of jeans, commando. He threw on a comfortable T-shirt, ran his fingers through his hair, and looked in the mirror at his perfect reflection.

Justin put on his Calvin Klein cotton boxers and his jeans and a Ralph Lauren shirt. As the new poster boy for the brand, Justin was never lacking in Polo gear.

"Thanks, man," Justin said to Dorian, who seemed to be hypnotized by his own visage. "Thanks for making that bearable. I mean . . . for helping me get through it."

"No problema," Dorian said. "Hey, you want to hang out? I know this great club across town. We can kick back and have some drinks and some fun before we have to catch that flight later on tomorrow."

"Sure. What's the club?"

"It's called the Hoist."

Justin had never been to a place like this: Men dressed in leather. Men wearing dog collars and leashes. Men in tight jeans. Businessmen, small men, white, black, Asian. Wall-to-wall men, shoulder to shoulder. Dorian noticed the puzzled look on Justin's face and burst out laughing.

"Yo, man, it's not funny," Justin said angrily. "I told you I'm not a fucking batty boy!"

"Relax, relax, my homophobic friend," Dorian said, wrapping his arm around Justin's shoulder.

Justin flicked Dorian off.

"I'm not afraid of anything. I'm just not like that. Why would you bring me here?"

"I just want to have some fun," Dorian said.

"At my expense?"

"No. I think if you loosen up, you will have some fun," Dorian said. "Just stick with me and no one will bother you. I think you will enjoy yourself, and new experiences will help to broaden your horizons."

"I don't need any new experiences!" Justin snapped.

"Look, this is who I am," Dorian said. "I don't want to shove it down your throat. And as I said before, I don't want to fuck you.

I'm not even attracted to you. But I think we could be friends. And any friend of mine will have to accept who I am and what I'm about. I want you to get to know me better. And I want to know what you're about."

"I'm not gay," Justin barked at him.

"I *know* you're not gay. We've established that. Now why don't you tell me the rest over a drink or two—my treat. Come on."

Justin didn't want to be a jerk. He was angry—or more scared, perhaps, if he really thought about it. While he always considered himself to be an open and accepting person, perhaps he wasn't. He cringed at the sight of men being sexual with each other, touching and kissing. It freaked him out more than a little.

"In Jamaica, men get killed for being gay," Justin told him. "It's completely frowned upon. The first time I was in Chelsea, I was mortified when I saw two men holding hands and walking their bulldog. I didn't get it. But at least that kind of activity was confined to certain neighborhoods. I've never seen anything like *this*, though," Justin said, looking at the crowd in the bar.

Justin was comfortable with homophobia. He was used to it. This—being in a club full of men who seemed not to give a damn what anybody thought—was going to take some getting used to. But he had taken a liking to Dorian. Justin thought he was cool and funny and he wanted to give him a chance. Maybe they could be friends.

As the evening progressed, Justin did loosen up quite a bit. He even hit the dance floor when one of his favorite house tunes, by Barbara Tucker, came on. He couldn't keep still in his seat.

"Come on, let's dance," Dorian said, grabbing Justin's arm and pulling him to the dance floor.

By this time the liquor was flowing through Justin's veins so strongly that he couldn't resist. He let the music take him.

Freedom!

Justin felt like he was flying. The dance floor was packed with shirtless, gyrating bodies, back to back, shoulder to shoulder. The driving, thumping baseline had Justin in a trance.

Justin's eyes were closed, and he was moving in a way that set Dorian's loins on fire. Dorian couldn't remember ever having seen someone move so effortlessly, so powerfully, so gracefully.

Justin was caught up, but so was Dorian, who couldn't keep his eyes off this man.

They walked across the river, back to their hotel. It was the most fun Justin could ever remember having. The night air did him good, as he was still feeling the aftereffects of one drink too many. But by the time they made it back to their hotel, Justin's head was still reeling.

Their rooms were across the hall from each other and Justin was having a hard time getting the key into his lock. He was still, but it was as if the entire hallway was spinning. He was breathing like he'd run a sprint.

"Are you okay, fella?" Dorian said, chuckling. "Maybe you shouldn't have had that last shot."

"I know," Justin said with a grin. "I will be all right, though."

"Do you need some help with that?" Dorian came over and grabbed the doorknob from behind and guided the key into Justin's lock. With his hand over Justin's he turned the knob and the two almost fell onto the floor as the door opened wide.

"Whoa," Dorian said, balancing Justin back upright.

The two were laughing at the clumsiness—a complete departure from their usual composure. Dorian didn't want to admit it, but he, too, was a bit tipsy. Dorian closed the door and got Justin to the couch. The room was a suite, with a couch and a television in the small living room area. Dorian guided him to the couch and Justin flopped down backward as Dorian toppled on top of him.

It was an awkward position, not unlike some of their poses earlier in the day. This time, with no cameras, Dorian did something he had been dying to do all night. He began to kiss Justin, first slowly and then feverishly. Without thinking, Justin reciprocated. When their tongues met, it was as if Justin had been zapped with a cattle prod. Somewhere it clicked in his head: *I am kissing a man! What the fuck?!*

Justin sobered up quickly—and pushed Dorian away.

"What's the matter?" said Dorian, genuinely puzzled.

"I can't," said Justin, so out of breath it felt as if his chest would explode. "I can't do this. I-I must be drunk. You have to go."

Dorian pulled himself off the couch and left.

The next day they rode to the airport without much conversation. The plane ride home was as silent as the plane ride there.

Dorian decided somewhere over the Atlantic that he wasn't going to bring it up. He also decided that he would have Justin—it was just a matter of time. He would wait. He was a very patient man. He would wait.

Justin would come to him in due time.

In his mind's eye

It was as if a switch had been turned on. I can't explain it, but something inside me is completely intrigued, completely consumed with wanting more of this feeling. I can't look at him without wanting to kiss him, wanting to just be near him, wanting to know what his scruffy beard will feel like on my face.

I cannot believe I am saying any of this. If you had told me that I would be attracted to a man, let alone imagine kissing him or imagine holding his throbbing dick in my hand—did I just think *that?—I would have said you were out of your fucking mind. But that is all I seem to be thinking about lately.*

I have to shake this off. I can't go down that road. I can't go down . . . I mean, what will that mean? I'm not gay. I don't want to be gay. A faggot? Hell no! Batty boy? Fuck no!

I'm ashamed to admit this, but back in Jamaica, we used to chase this one boy, Travis, when I was in the seventh grade. Every day, we would chase him home. Boy, could he run. One day, we were able to catch him. There were five of us and we caught up with him after he stumbled, cutting through the woods on the other side of his house.

I don't even know what I was doing with this group. I hated groups after this. I hated hanging out with anyone.

Travis was very effeminate. The kind of effeminate that was noticeable even when he was three. It wasn't that he played with dolls or hung out with the girls way too much—which he did. It wasn't that he was very thin and petite—which he was. It was how he talked. I could never understand how every gay guy I knew back then had that same way of talking. It was how he talked with his hands, flicking his wrist around in a way that made it seem game.

He was just born gay, like the song says, "from a little bitty boy . . . just a little bitty boy." In Jamaica, that can be a death sentence—or definitely an ass-whipping session.

I wasn't one of the ringleaders. I was just tagging along, a follower. These boys were determined to teach Travis a lesson for having the nerve to look at one of our crew. I was just tagging along. I'm sure now that Travis didn't look at anyone in that way. He was very careful to keep to himself. I doubt he even looked at anyone at all. But Ralph was determined to "show that batty boy bumbahole a lesson."

I was running, staying with the pack. I probably could have caught Travis at any point. I was pretty fast. But I didn't really want to catch him. And I had no idea what I would really do if and when Travis was caught.

But I got to find out. Why did he have to get caught in the woods? Ralph got to Travis first, delivering a kick to his belly that may have instantly broken a rib. He then pressed him down with his knee, pinning him to the ground, covering his mouth while the others piled on. Someone grabbed a huge stick, while another pulled down Travis's pants and rammed the stick in his ass with full force. The muffled screams were horrific. I wanted to scream, too, but I was busy helping hold him down. After that, Travis stopped struggling. He must have given up, and without much fight, Ralph and the others decided to let go.

As we were turning to leave, Ralph decided to add insult to injury. He took his dick out and peed all over Travis's face.

"And don't you ever look at me or any of my boys again, you little faggot," Ralph said, hawking and spitting on Travis before casually walking out of the woods as if nothing had happened. I remembered the satisfied look on Ralph's face and wondered if he felt nothing.

When I got home, I vomited.

I was sickened by what I had seen and what I had done. I carried that around for a while, especially when Travis never came back to school. His mother sent him away to a private school on the other side of the island. I decided not to tag along after that.

I decided to roll alone.

So it's quite ironic that I am now contemplating having sex with a man—did I just say that? *I must be losing it. I know I'm losing it. I could never go through with this. Snap the fuck out of it, Justin. Straighten up!*

Tasha, Tasha, Tasha, Tasha. Let me just get my ass home and fuck Tasha the way she wants to be fucked and forget about all this. Let me get home and take care of my woman.

My woman.

My woman.

My woman . . .

Chapter Twelve

With Justin in London, Tasha wanted to pour herself into her work—and she had a lot of it to do. She had neglected a few things over the past few weeks. Now she was staring at a deadline, a very critical deadline that could make or break her next season in business.

Tasha ran her fingers through her hair and sighed. She had been through what seemed like a hundred shots already and they were all a disappointment.

"I can't do this anymore!" she said. "I'm done."

Tasha looked around her office and noticed for the first time that they were in complete darkness. The sun had set hours ago and the only light was coming from the contact table.

"Anne, I need you to pull another one out of your hat for me," said Tasha as she got up, her palms to her eyes, to sit in one of the cube-shaped leather chairs in front of her desk.

Anne was a creative consultant for various magazines. She was the one responsible for choosing which models would grace the big fashion magazines. Anne had been living out of the Reynolds Agency for the past two weeks in an effort to produce a new-model catalog, which was sure to put Tasha's models on the cover of every major magazine for the spring line.

Tasha loved and admired how hard Anne worked for herself. Perhaps it was Tasha seeing so much of herself in Anne—or what Tasha always knew she could be. Anne was the best. Like Tasha, she was her own boss. Anne had carved out a niche for herself in one of the toughest industries to crack. And she'd made a mint doing so. Everything about Anne was top notch—including her look. She *always* looked good. Anne was never a model herself—never wanted to be—but she had all the qualities of an androgynous beauty.

On this night, Anne was going to earn every dime Tasha was paying her. Part of what made her so valuable to people was that she always came through. Anne never missed a deadline. She always predicted correctly. Anne knew how important it was for the Reynolds models to capture most of the major magazine covers—it would solidify Tasha as a major force in the industry. Anne wanted to see her there.

"I think you gave up too soon," Anne prodded Tasha. "I found some really great stuff here. You are supposed to enjoy this part of the business. No, you're supposed to *love* this, Ms. Reynolds."

"I know, I know," Tasha said, stretching her legs out in front of her, getting in a good yawn. "I'm just tired and I've been burning the candle at both ends. I'll be able to attack this first thing in the morning."

"Yeah, but this needs to go to print first thing in the morning, Tasha. We can't still be working on this in the morning. We must choose the best model and also forecast what the new look will be for next year."

"Okay, how about we take a one-hour break," said Tasha. "It's only ten thirty; we can certainly be done by twelve. What do you think?"

Anne walked over to where Tasha was sitting and kneeled down in front of her while Tasha was still trying to negotiate her way out of working. Anne wanted to get a better look at this woman who knew full well that they didn't have time for a break.

Tasha looked up and didn't realize how close Anne was. In that same moment she was stunned by how beautiful Anne was. Even in the half shadows of the darkened room, there was a radiance to Anne's face. She was five years Tasha's senior but actually looked younger.

"You know what we have to do," Anne said, looking directly into Tasha's eyes.

Tasha knew that Anne was talking to her, but she found herself almost mesmerized by this woman, comforted by this woman, and downright aroused by this woman.

"Listen, I'm not tired," Anne continued. "I can finish the selection by myself. That *is* what you're paying me to do, so let me do my job."

Anne casually reached up and put some of Tasha's hair behind her ear.

Tasha continued to stare, amazed by what a black woman and a German man had produced.

"Why are you staring at me like that?" said Anne. "Oh, wait a minute. I know that look."

"What look?" said Tasha.

"No need to be defensive, because I thought the same thing about you all night," Anne said. "Okay, who am I fooling . . . all week. But then I said to myself, 'Anne, it's not worth it and it will never work; she still wants to play like a lady.' "

Tasha was shocked.

"Wait . . . you, you think that I . . ."

Before Tasha could say another word, Anne had leaned in and occupied the air and opportunity between them. Tasha's mouth and body were responding in a way that was more natural than she wanted to believe. It was amazing to Tasha how good Anne smelled.

Anne pulled her gently to the floor and Tasha went willingly as Anne lay on top of her, never letting their lips separate. The deep, thick, almond-colored shag rug that Tasha never allowed anyone to walk on provided the perfect backdrop to a long session of wonderful and completely fulfilling lovemaking.

Tasha woke up just after dawn, the sun streaming in a beam across her office. She awoke refreshed, with clear thoughts, renewed energy, and memories of the night before. She rolled over on the long pillow that had been taken from the couch. It still smelled of Anne and she couldn't help but smile. Anne smelled expensive and scrumptious.

The phone startled Tasha out of her dream state. She bolted upright and made it to her desk to see that it was nearly seven o'clock.

"Anne? Hi . . ." Tasha cleared her throat and sat in silence, not knowing what to say.

"Good morning, love!" Anne said. "I just wanted to let you know that I have selected the proofs and I'm going to take them to the printer in about an hour. I locked your office door, so take comfort in the fact that no one can barge in before you get yourself together."

As she adjusted the headpiece on her phone, Anne handed the keys to her Bentley sport to the valet of her building and rushed to the elevator being held for her by the doorman.

"Tasha, I just want to say that I had a beautiful time last night, and I couldn't sleep," she said. "I have all kinds of nervous energy right now, so I'm going to use it to get a lot of work done."

"Thanks, Anne," Tasha said, still unsure as to whether she should talk about their night together. "I'll talk with you later."

Tasha put down the phone, snapped her bra, which had the clasp in the front, and buttoned her blouse. She was in deep thought. They were thoughts she couldn't quite sort out. Tasha was confused.

What just happened?

And is it going to happen again?

Across town, handling another part of Tasha's business, Anne held the phone, not wanting to let go of Tasha. She finally passed her thumb over the smooth surface of her iPhone, allowing the unit to go black. Anne couldn't stop thinking about the divine Ms. Reynolds. She, too, had more to say but didn't. Anne wanted to tell Tasha that she didn't wake her up because she would have wanted to make love to her again and again. But there was work to be done. Besides, the office would shortly fill with the mail-room people, then the assistants, secretaries, and agents. So she left.

She left before both of them got into even more trouble.

Anne wanted to tell Tasha so many things—things she knew she might never get to utter. But she was content to hold on to the memory of that night and content to never bring it up again, even if it was just that once.

Chapter Thirteen

Anne knew she was nervous when she couldn't decide what to wear to an all-too-common Fashion Week event.

She was impressed with the entire line she had to choose from. Darryl Brown had sent it to her. His taste was impeccable and he loved dressing her. The truth was, it didn't matter which outfit she selected, because the beautiful creams and browns that he'd picked out were all elegant and stylish.

Anne remembered her early years in the business, when she couldn't afford the lifestyle that currently surrounded her. She remembered trying to break into this crazy business with all of its glamour, glitz, and pressure. She remembered how immediately enamored she'd been with it all.

Unlike most women in the fashion industry, Anne Becker never wanted to be a model. She detested the thought of it. She wanted to create the stars, but never be one. With her artistic eye and businesslike manner, she fast became the trusted mind for every magazine editor and modeling agency alike.

It was Darryl Brown who'd helped solidify Anne as the one. The two had met more than a decade before, when Anne, on her first assignment as a creative consultant, showed up an hour early—her usual punctual self—for a fashion show.

"Come, quick, I need you!" Darryl was in a tizzy because two of his models were running late and he had to do a run-through of his line to see how the clothes hung.

"All we need to do is go through the motions on this," he said. "Put those clothes on!"

Anne hesitated. She couldn't imagine that he was talking to her.

"Come on, baby girl, we don't have all day!" said an exasperated Darryl. "God knows you have the look and the body to pull it off. Come, come!"

"Okay. Of course I'll do it," said Anne as she put her briefcase down and began to undress right in front of Darryl.

"So what do I get to put on first?" Anne pointed to the wardrobe full of clothes.

"Cue the music and the lights!" shouted Darryl to the deejay backstage. "I want you to put on everything!"

Anne dressed and undressed more times than she could remember, enjoying the playful banter with Darryl.

"Work it, girl! Damn, you're beautiful! Are you sure you want to stay behind the scenes?"

Darryl shouted, clapped, and hooted each time Anne came

from behind the curtain in a different outfit, making each look better than the last. Anne's thick, curly hair grew wilder and wilder as she walked under the hot lights.

"I don't know too many black women with nappy dirty blond hair," Darryl said. "But you are *killing* it."

Anne's hair was parted down the middle and hung down her back. By the end of the night, it looked like one of Diana Ross's wigs. Darryl told one of the grips to bring him a camera. He said he needed proof that the best-looking model in New York City wasn't even looking for work.

After the shoot, Anne invited Darryl back to her small one-bedroom apartment on the Lower East Side and Darryl graciously accepted. The apartment was sparsely furnished, but the things she did have were of outstanding quality and style. Darryl admired the hand-carved wooden coffee table that had been shipped from Germany. It had belonged to her father's mother.

Anne brought an elegant sterling-silver tray out of her kitchen, placed it on the coffee table, and joined Darryl on the uniquely long navy-blue leather ottoman backed with blue-and-white-striped pillows.

"So how long do you plan on living here, Anne?" Darryl asked.

"Oh, the people here are wonderful. Don't believe the hype," she said. "I no longer *need* to live here. I'm doing well for myself. Actually, I work every day of the week now and my consulting jobs are lasting a lot longer. Most of the magazines are asking me to stay on permanently at great salaries. But I only want to work for myself. I think turning them down makes them want me more."

"But it's the *Loisiada*!" Darryl said, turning up his nose. "It's not even Chelsea, Tribeca, or Soho. It's time to move!"

"In due time," she said, chuckling. "The thing you need to know about me is that I plan everything—*everything*—in my life. I purposely keep my lifestyle and expenses low so that when I make my move, it will be for good. You'd be amazed by how much you can do without when you have a bigger picture to focus on."

"That's just too much focusing, girl. You need to *live,*" Darryl said. "Life is short. I don't plan. I just live my dreams. I like making and designing clothes. I didn't plan it; I just knew I couldn't do anything else."

Darryl and Anne talked and drank coffee until the sun came up. And they were close friends ever since.

Now she debated telling Darryl about her encounter with Tasha.

I know I will see her. I have to keep my cool.

The intercom buzzer jarred her out of her thoughts. It was the doorman announcing Darryl's arrival. They had made it their business to do at least one Fashion Week show when they were both in town.

She was waiting at the door for him as he got off the elevator.

"Oh no! Why aren't you dressed?" he said, looking at his Breitling watch. "Oh my gosh!"

Darryl knew Anne too well.

"You are *never* nervous," he said. "You *are* style. So you're either meeting someone for the first time—and that wouldn't even be an issue with you—or . . . there is someone you are trying to impress. 'Fess up! Who is it?"

Darryl folded his arms, opened his eyes wide, and tapped his foot.

"Who is it?!" he shouted. "Who is it! Who is it!"

Anne couldn't stop laughing at Darryl's antics.

"No, I'm serious!" said Darryl, laying Anne's outfits out for her and forcing her to get dressed. "Okay, you aren't saying? Fine! You know I will find out. Now sit down so I can do your hair."

Darryl began to undo the cornrows that lined her head, creating beautiful curly locks.

"Okay, now put something on your lips," he said. "You don't need makeup. You're beautiful. Let's go! We're late."

When Darryl and Anne got downstairs, her Bentley Continental GT was waiting for them.

Chapter Fourteen

Is there a problem?" Tasha said as she gathered together the sheets around her and sat upright in bed. "Is it something I said? What's up?"

She tried to make light of it, but since Justin had come back from London they had made love only once—that first night he'd gotten back. It was ferocious, as if Justin was eating a meal for the first time after having been starving. It was incredible. But as good as it was, Tasha could sense that there was something. She couldn't put her finger on it. But something was amiss.

"Come on now, you're perfect," Justin said, trying to assure her as he wrapped his arms around her and scooted her back down. "There's nothing wrong. I guess I'm tired. Still jet-lagged."

"It's been a week. I've flown all over the world and I know jet lag doesn't last that long," Tasha said. "Whatever it is, I can handle it. Whatever you need to talk about, I'm here for you."

Tasha had some things she needed to talk about, too. But there was no way she was going to bring any of that up. Anne. It was simple enough. Whatever Tasha was feeling—and she was definitely feeling something—she would stuff and bury, the way she always did. End of story.

"Well, whatever it is or isn't, you had better get it together!" Tasha said. "Mama's not going to put up with too many more of what happened last night."

Justin hadn't slept the night before. He'd spent the evening staring at the ceiling, thinking about Dorian. Thoughts of that white man were on the verge of consuming him. But he couldn't talk about it. He knew it wasn't fair to Tasha. She didn't deserve not to get his all. She had done so much for him and he owed her. More than that, he loved her. He *still* loved her. He was so confused.

He grabbed Tasha around the waist and held on to her as she cradled his head in her lap.

"I love you," he said.

"I love you, too," she said.

With his face buried in her lap, she couldn't tell for sure, but she thought for a moment that Justin was crying.

He fell asleep just like that, his head in her lap.

Chapter Fifteen

Love.

Tasha had no clue as to what that word meant. She had a picture of the scripture for "love," found in the thirteenth chapter of 1 Corinthians, verses 4 through 8. It started, "Love is patient, love is kind . . ." She'd picked it up in a Bed, Bath & Beyond several years before, when she was going through her "spiritual phase."

That phase didn't last long, as Tasha realized that the principles of following Christ didn't quite mesh with the world she thought she wanted. Hermès and Gucci; Mercedes and penthouses; power, control, and opulence weren't the kinds of things that fit in with giving everything to the poor and serving God. So Tasha decided that serving her current master—who she thought was herself—was serving her well.

She was successful, she was rich, and she was powerful. And now the only missing piece in her life was here. Finally. He was with her every night, tucking her in, rubbing her neck and her feet, taking baths with her, making wonderful love to her.

"Love." *There's that word again.*

Did she love Justin? Or did she love what Justin represented? Did she love the man or did she love the man she had created for the public and in her own image? Did she love Anne? Not that any of that mattered, because Anne didn't fit into the world Tasha had created for herself. That place was reserved for Justin.

"And whatever is going on, I'm going to fix it," she said to herself. "Should we make this official? Am I moving too fast?"

Tasha had few doubts in her life. But this was one time when she seemed to doubt everything. She didn't know whether she was coming or going, and the toughest part was suppressing the chaos that was brewing inside her. No one could see this side of her. She had to keep it pulled together.

The other sad thing was that the only other person she could talk to about it—actually the only two people on this earth she would share this with—she couldn't. Anne was one of her best friends, the one person she could count on to give her a straight answer, no chaser. The one person who would have an answer for her was one of the reasons Tasha was so confused.

And Justin, her confidant. She couldn't tell him what she was feeling. Part of the mystique of their relationship, Tasha believed, was her ability to appear flawless and damn near perfect most of the time. When Tasha did show a vulnerable side of herself, it was completely calculated.

What was her next move? Keep Justin happy and keep Anne away from her. Stick and move.

She got a Brazilian wax at her favorite salon, to go with her weekly pedicure. She stopped by Saks and picked up a new negligee. While they weren't known for it, Saks had some of the classiest, sexiest lingerie. She ordered food from Justin's favorite restaurant. She lit the candles and set the table.

Justin was out on another shoot for Polo, which was going to feature him in their latest billboard ad in Times Square. He was expected to be home around eight and Tasha wanted the evening to be perfect. She pulled out the scented oils, which would be used after their sensuous bath. She was amazed by how much Justin liked to sit in the tub. Most men preferred a hop into the shower. Actually, Tasha wasn't a big bath person, until Justin had come along. He loved to soak at least twice a week. And that became part of their routine.

Tasha made sure she had the biggest and best tub because that's just the way she did things. She wanted to make sure she had the best, even if she didn't use it often—like her cars. She knew she could drive only one at a time, and mostly she was driven. But Tasha had to have the show cars. She had to have the show man in Justin because she needed her show life.

Tasha was going to seduce Justin tonight. She was going to satisfy him. She was going to make him happy.

The mood was perfect. After dinner, Tasha handed Justin a red box with a black bow on it.

"What's this?" he said.

"Open it," she said, smiling.

Justin took the top off the box, which was big enough for a fancy watch. But once he opened it, he discovered a key inside. He looked at her, puzzled. Tasha grabbed him by the hand and led him outside the building and to the garage. And there, sitting in the front, was a brand-new Lexus SC 430 hardtop convertible in silver, with black interior and Coach leather seats.

"Wow! I can't accept this," he said.

"You sure can, because you paid for it," Tasha said, smiling.

"What do you mean?" he asked.

"So do you think all of those photo shoots and fashion shows that you've appeared in for the last half of the year have been for free?" Tasha said. "You have *more* than earned this."

"What if I didn't want a car?" he said, thinking about how he would really like to spend his money.

"Then consider it a gift from me," Tasha said. "I want you to have it. A top model has to travel in style."

"It's too much," he said. "I would much rather put that money in the bank."

"Okay, take it for a spin and if you still feel the same way, we'll take it back to the dealer," she said, deciding that they could have a bath and more later. After riding in the car, he would be more inclined to ride her all night long.

Tasha knew that once he got behind that wheel and felt one of the smoothest, sexiest rides ever, he would thank her for being so thoughtful. No man on earth could refuse good sex or a good ride.

Justin had made close to $150,000 in just a little over six months. Tasha didn't actually use Justin's money to buy the car. It was a token of her appreciation, and he had earned it. His money was being kept for him in a trust. He'd basically signed over all control to Tasha when he joined her agency. He trusted her with his money. But perhaps he would have to rethink things like the purchase of the car without Tasha's having asked him.

He didn't like being dependent on her. He didn't like being dependent on anyone. That's why he'd chosen to sell cane on the street—even if it was at his father's demand—instead of taking a comfortable job at the home office. He liked being his own man, calling his own shots. And, for a while, he accepted deferring to Tasha because he knew he had so much to learn. As a stranger in a strange land, it was best for Justin to keep quiet and learn. But his role was wearing thin because he wasn't being authentically himself.

At times he felt like Tasha's boy toy—an accessory, like one of her handbags or a pair of shoes. Other times he felt like her man, the love of her life. But even in that role, Tasha liked to be in control. Everything had to be her way.

Tasha's latest project was pushing him to apply for citizenship. She said it would make it easier for him in the long run, especially if he wanted to buy a place of his own. Everything couldn't be in her name. But this was one area where Justin balked. He loved his country. He was proud to be a Jamaican. He liked the values he'd been raised with; now, little by little, he felt like he was losing himself.

Justin resisted as much as he could. He didn't want to buy into Tasha's world of materialism, but when he sat in that Lexus, it exceeded his wildest dreams. It didn't take long for him to see himself behind the wheel. Tasha wasn't making it easy for him on so many fronts. But it wasn't easy for him to lose the things he loved about himself.

And then there was this relationship he had with her. What

was it, exactly? What were they to each other? Was he simply her creation, something to be shown around to the world? Or did he really mean something to her? Did he really love her, or was it gratitude?

She wasn't making it easy for him to sort it all out—especially not with surprises like the one he was sitting in.

"So are you going to take me for a ride or what?" said Tasha. "I was thinking we could ride through Central Park and then head down Broadway. That is one of the most beautiful rides at night—almost as beautiful as that ride on the upper level of the George Washington Bridge. Are you up to that?"

Justin had to admit it—he liked the feel behind that wheel. He sat there not knowing which button to push first. He reached for the button that would drop the roof.

"Wait! What are you doing?" asked Tasha. "We can't ride with the top down! That would destroy my hair!"

"Are you kidding? How can we *not* put the top down?" Justin saw that Tasha didn't appreciate his comment; she didn't like to be challenged or contradicted. She didn't say anything, but he knew it was best to leave the roof up. So he did.

The rest of the ride was filled with questions, questions that annoyed Justin, but he tried to enjoy the smooth ride and tune her out.

"Did you go to the gym today?" she asked.

She didn't wait for him to answer, because it was so important for him to stay at his best, especially now. More and more requests for Justin were coming in. And Tasha was planning to make their relationship public at just the right time—maybe with an engagement announcement. She continued to talk, not sure if he understood that her reputation was on the line with everything he did and that she could not be crossed.

By the time Tasha finished directing him with a "Turn right here!" and a "Take a left at the light!" they'd ended up at the entrance to the bridge.

"I don't have any money for the toll coming back," Justin said. "So we're going to Jersey and then what?"

"We'll turn around and come back," she said. "I have a nightcap waiting for you back at home. Let's pull over and put the top down. Fuck my hair!"

Justin looked at her, puzzled. She'd been so adamant about not putting down the top, and surly about it. Now she wanted the top down and seemed very happy. She grabbed his free hand as he used the other to put down the hardtop.

Justin was convinced she had multiple personalities, like Sybil or some sort of female Jekyll and Hyde.

Chapter Sixteen

After their drive, Justin was exhilarated. He came back and serviced Tasha the way she hadn't been serviced in quite some time. They even skipped the bath. Tasha slept like a baby. But Justin was restless. He couldn't sleep. He wanted to be happy that Tasha seemed so happy with him. But he wasn't. He was fidgety.

Before the sun broke through the darkness, Justin slipped out of bed, threw on a pair of shorts, an Under Armour shirt, a hooded sweatshirt, clipped on his iPod shuffle, and went for a three-mile run. Justin loved running through the streets of New York. He said it felt like he was in a real jungle, because he never knew what to expect—dodging cabbies, dog shit, and rude pedestrians. It was a hard, fast run and Justin felt better afterward.

On his way back home, he stopped at the local Starbucks. Standing at the counter, paying for a mocha latte, was Dorian.

"What are you doing here?" Justin asked, looking surprised.

"I live a few blocks away," Dorian said.

"So we're neighbors?"

"I guess we are," said Dorian, who looked at Justin as if he wanted to devour him.

Justin felt his skin flush. If his skin were lighter, Dorian would have noticed him blushing. They stood there for a few moments, not speaking a word but saying a lot. Their protons and neutrons and electrons seemed to have minds of their own, crashing into one another with reckless abandon. Justin felt as if he was being touched all over his body even though there was plenty of physical space between them. He had never felt anything like it in his life.

"So why don't you stop by sometime?" Dorian said.

The two of them had not connected since that time in London. And Justin chalked that up to being in a foreign country with too much to drink. He dismissed that whole experience and tried to pretend it had never happened. So when they touched back onto American soil, Justin ran as far from Dorian and that experience in London as he could. He ran back to his life, the life he had with Tasha.

But it seemed like he was running from more than Dorian. And it had finally caught him. As he stood at the Starbucks counter, nervously, anxiously, Justin knew *he* was caught.

"Sure, why not?" Justin said.

"What about tonight? I just bought a really nice bottle of wine you might enjoy," Dorian said. "Around seven thirty?"

"Okay," Justin said before he could even think about it. What *was* he thinking about? How was he going over to Dorian's? What would he say to Tasha?

He decided he would say nothing.

So that evening, when he showered and put on running gear again, all Tasha said as he was leaving was, "Glad to see you're putting some work in on that million-dollar body. Now that's my man!"

"I'll be back soon," Justin yelled back as he closed the door.

He got to Dorian's in less than three minutes, nervous energy propelling him. Dorian buzzed him up. Justin took the stairs, seven flights up. He got to the door and stood there for an eternity. Before he could knock, the door swung open.

"Are you just going to stand out there all night?" Dorian said with a grin.

A startled Justin came in. His heart was racing and he was sure that Dorian could hear it. Dorian seemed so confident, so sure of himself and the situation. He offered Justin a seat at the island in his kitchen.

Justin marveled at Dorian's decor—everything was white, including a unique whiteish granite top on the island and counters. Justin hadn't realized there were so many variations of the color, from cream to vanilla to bone white. The walls were a rice-paper white, which Dorian said had a hint of black in the mix.

"I special-ordered it," Dorian said proudly.

Dorian opened the bottle of wine he'd used as an incentive for Justin to come. But Justin hadn't come for the wine. He took a sip and let the fruity bouquet erupt in his mouth. Justin didn't want to move from the kitchen with the glass of red wine. He imagined himself spilling it on the white Berber carpeting in the living room. So he just sat there and sipped.

"So how are you enjoying this business of ours?" Dorian said, making small talk as he cut up some cheese and placed some crackers on the plate with it.

"It's okay," Justin said. "Not at all what I expected."

"What did you expect?"

"I don't know, just not this."

Dorian walked out of the kitchen and led Justin into the living room.

"Let me give you the grand tour," he said. "You can take your glass with you."

Justin decided to leave it, following Dorian around the massive apartment. It wasn't as big as Tasha's, but it had high ceilings, white oak floors buffed to perfection, and lots of space. Dorian was a minimalist and didn't have much furniture or artwork.

"As you can see, I like things simple," he said, showing Justin the bedroom that he'd turned into a workout room. It had a treadmill, a sit-up bench, and free weights.

"You can come over any time and use the equipment," Dorian said. "Since that Abercrombie ad outside the Lincoln Tunnel, I get noticed a lot at the gym. Usually, I love the attention, but not when I'm sweaty and not at my best."

Justin chuckled at Dorian's vanity.

They walked into the master bedroom. It was like a walk into heaven. The down-filled white Wamsutta comforter covered a bed that had an ivory headboard.

"It was my father's. He had it made before they outlawed harvesting ivory," Dorian said. "Or maybe he had it done in spite of the ban. I don't remember. But isn't it beautiful?"

It was incredible. Justin had never seen anything like it. He felt as if he could dive into that king-size bed and simply float, like he were on a cloud.

Justin stood just inside the doorway. Dorian came up behind him. Justin could feel his breath on his neck. Justin turned around and was face-to-face with Dorian. They both stood just over six feet tall. Dorian stroked Justin's face. And Justin surprised himself, letting out a low moan. Dorian grabbed Justin's hand and squeezed it. Justin thought he would hit the floor as his knees buckled underneath him. He'd never thought that someone holding his hand could give him such a rush.

With his free hand, Justin grabbed the back of Dorian's head and pulled him close. The kiss was even better than the first time. The two moved to the bed without separating. Within minutes the two were naked, on top of the covers. Justin's dark brown skin looked like a giant slab of melted chocolate against the white bed.

As they kissed and stroked each other, a million thoughts ran through Justin's mind. Not one of those thoughts said, "Stop!" He couldn't stop himself anyway. And while he had never done this before, it was the most natural thing he had ever done. Every move, every touch seemed orchestrated for just the two of them.

Can this man read my mind?

Just when he thought he couldn't take any more and was wondering what was going to happen next, Dorian gently tried to roll Justin over on his stomach.

What the fuck? Justin thought to himself. He wasn't quite ready for that. He twisted around and Dorian gently touched him and said, "It's okay. Trust me."

It's pretty hard to trust a man standing over you with a huge erection and wanting to turn you over on your stomach, Justin thought.

The one thing Justin knew for sure was that he *never* wanted a man to penetrate him. That was just *too* gay. And Justin, even in the arms of this man, kissing and licking and stroking this man, didn't consider himself gay.

Justin rolled over reluctantly. He was nervous and scared. But he trusted Dorian, who reached over to his nightstand and pulled out something. It was a straw, which he gently inserted between Justin's cheeks and blew. It was a sensation that Justin had never felt before and he instantly shot his creamy come all over Dorian's creamy sheets. Dorian reignited the flame in Justin's loins by replacing the straw with his tongue. He gave Justin the first rim job he had ever had, sucking Justin's tight balls from behind while stroking his huge dick until he came a second time.

Justin thought he had absolutely lost his mind. He couldn't catch his breath. Trembling, Justin turned over and pushed Dorian onto his back. He was possessed. He didn't take his time, nor did he bother with the soft, gentle play. Justin grabbed Dorian's dick with a force and took it all in his mouth. The taste of another's penis filled Justin with an insatiable hunger. He devoured every inch of Dorian's bulging purple member until Dorian's eyes nearly rolled back in his head.

Dorian grabbed the sheets with all of his might as he bucked and let out a primal moan. Justin tasted the strange come for the first time and it was sweet, like nectar. He lapped up every bit and wanted more.

Justin was sprung.

In his mind's eye

I never imagined myself being with a man. But now that I am, I can honestly say I can never imagine myself being with anyone but a man ever again. It is the most natural thing I could ever do. It's as natural as waking up, as eating.

To feel somebody who feels just like me. To have someone who knows me without my ever uttering a word—to know how I feel inside, to know my innermost thoughts. And sexually, to know every single spot on my body that will drive me absolutely crazy. It's incredible. If someone had told me that it would feel like this, I would not have wasted so many years trying to be something other than this.

Gay? Yes, I am happy—happier than I have ever been. I know it's not just Dorian. If Dorian were a woman, I know I wouldn't feel this way. And don't get me wrong, I love women—I still do. I love their softness, their roundness in certain places. I love the way they smell—that unique scent of a woman still can make me hard. But when I think about total fulfillment, when I think about completion, I think of Dorian.

Dorian is soft, too. Or, more smooth than soft. His big, knowing hands are like bear paws—strong, yet soft. Like a surgeon's, knowing exactly what to do.

When he comes near me, I get butterflies in anticipation. Butterflies! Over a man! I'm having a hard time coming to grips with it all. But I'm having a harder time controlling myself, controlling my feelings. But I must control my feelings. I cannot let this get out of hand.

Tasha doesn't deserve this.

Shit. Shit. Shit!

She doesn't deserve to be with someone who has changed, who's not totally there anymore. She deserves to have someone who wants to be with her 100 percent.

I have to tell her. But how? How in the hell am I going to tell Tasha, "I'm in love with a man"?

How can I tell her something like that when I can't even say it to myself?

Chapter Seventeen

Dorian had ten minutes to get ready for his next date. It was becoming a chore to keep up with everyone. He was juggling two women and an assortment of men and doing so with the deft agility of a panther. Dorian had always been very popular. Even in high school, he was a player. He had two dates to his senior prom. He couldn't make up his mind. One was the head cheerleader, the other the student body president. Dorian had so much charm that he was able to convince both young ladies to go with him. No one was surprised when he walked into the school's auditorium in his white tuxedo and white bow tie, two of the most beautiful girls in his school on either arm.

He was the man then, and his influence only increased as he

became more and more successful. As a recognized face, with money and time between jobs, Dorian needed the variety to keep him from being bored. So on Mondays he was with Rachel—an Elite model he'd met on the set of his first Paris *Vogue* shoot. He would extend their time together into Tuesday if neither of them was working and he still wanted to be with her beyond that one night. Hump day, Wednesday, was his cruising night. He would hit Washington Square Park or Chelsea Pier, dressed way down in beat-up jeans and a wool hat and a few days' worth of stubble.

Dorian looked forward to Wednesdays. It was his chance to be absolutely naughty and anonymous. At first he loved being seen and being known. He still enjoyed it, but he wanted it on his terms. With his proclivity for men, it made it difficult for him to really live his life the way he wanted to. He did a lot of hiding out and pretending and he hated it. But on Wednesdays he got to be totally free, albeit in disguise. He was this faceless, nameless, sexy body who could do whatever he wanted. And he did.

Sometimes there were no condoms used in those secret places throughout the park. He would give and receive mind-blowing blow jobs in places like the disgusting park restroom. But he was in his glory. Nobody asked him any questions. He didn't have to talk much, pose, flex, or be on his game. He didn't even have to shower if he didn't want to. They closed his favorite bathhouse, off of Twenty-third Street. But he hadn't really been able to go there without being recognized.

The wonderful thing about the gay community in New York was that while there was a faction eager to out any and everyone, there was still very much a code of honor and secrecy. Local television stars could walk freely on Fire Island with their lovers and the mainstream public had no clue. They could host national, nightly entertainment shows while being known as the biggest whores around, coworkers and others clueless. So being spotted in a bathhouse wasn't the worst thing. But having anonymous sex in the park was the absolute best thing for Dorian.

Heading into the weekend, Dorian might hang out with Veronica, a beautiful Portuguese hostess at an upscale midtown restaurant. She was always on call for Dorian and he enjoyed barhopping with her. She could drink most men under the table and her wild style kept him interested.

But now it was Justin—his chocolate-covered man toy he seemed to be uncovering the whole world for. He was so bright eyed (beautiful, hazel-colored bright eyes), so naive, so refreshing, with such an almost childlike innocence. Dorian looked forward to being with Justin the way he looked forward to his Wednesdays, only it was different—the exact opposite. Wednesdays were completely impersonal and all about sex. With Justin it was completely personal and not so much about the sex. That personal connection made the sex incredible for Dorian, who had spent most of his life not getting close to anyone.

The Bang & Olufsen BeoCom phone chirped. It was the only thing in his apartment that wasn't white.

"Hey, it's me, Justin," the voice on the other end said. "You up for some company?"

Tasha was out for the evening, so Justin took this opportunity to be with Dorian again. Living with Tasha and working with Tasha made it virtually impossible for Justin to steal away without suspicion. He could continue to go on his nightly "runs," but Justin wasn't too sure how long it would be before Tasha figured out what he was really running toward.

It had been a few days since Justin and Dorian had had sex for the first time. They had talked a couple of times, but neither really knew what to say or where it was all going. Justin had left without saying much. And Dorian was never one for many words. But he knew he couldn't stop thinking about Justin.

"Sure, come on over," Dorian said. He checked his watch. Veronica was supposed to meet him at the Mercer Hotel in Soho. He was already running late. He would call her on her cell and tell her they'd have their rendezvous another night. Dorian loved that Veronica never put any pressure on him and was always down for whatever, whenever. Not at all like Rachel. If Dorian had canceled on her at the last minute, he wouldn't hear from her for weeks. She would eventually step back in line, but Dorian would have to work extra hard. He didn't mind, because he loved how they looked together. She was his perfect on-the-town companion. She lived up to all appearances.

His buzzer rang about five minutes after hanging up with Justin.

"What the fuck, man? Did you literally run over here?" Dorian asked after opening the door and letting Justin in.

"I was actually downstairs," he said. "I've been walking around the city. I really need to talk to you."

Dorian sank into his plush couch, one bare foot planted on the seat. Justin sat down next to him. He wanted to reach out, caress Dorian's hand, just touch him. But he kept his space.

"I can't stop thinking about you," Justin said. "I don't know what this is. But it's really complicating things."

Dorian didn't respond. He kept a stoic expression and simply listened.

"Well, I have this thing with Tasha, and I'm really grateful for everything she's done for me, but I don't know if I can keep it up," Justin said.

"What do you mean?" Dorian said, finally breaking his own silence.

"I mean I can't be with her anymore," Justin said. "I can't sleep with her anymore. When I think of being touched, I think of you."

"That's a good thing," Dorian chuckled. "So why don't you just think of me when you're making love to her. Role-play in your mind. Let what we do—or what you want me to do to you—carry you over until you can get the real thing. Why mess that up?"

"I feel like a fucking liar, Dorian," he said. "How in the world can I fuck Tasha and tell her 'I love you' when I don't mean it? It's just not right."

"Well, I know one thing. It won't be right if you tell her the truth. That's for sure!" Dorian said. "Maybe you've never seen this side of her, but Tasha can be a fucking bitch. I mean a *real* bitch! Tell her the truth, if you want to, but please leave my name out of it. I have seen her completely destroy at least two people—and I don't think she was even sleeping with them. She blacklisted them right out of modeling for talking behind her back. Imagine what she'd do to you, and me too? So, please, leave my name out of it."

Justin was a little stung. He thought Dorian felt the same way he did.

"Don't worry, I won't mention you at all," Justin shot back. "This is *my* problem. But don't you ever get tired of hiding and lying?"

"Sure I do . . . sometimes," said Dorian, realizing how much of an ass he'd just been. "But I make a game of it. Look, as much as all of this is becoming more and more acceptable, I'm still not willing to just tell the world, 'Look at me! I'm gay!' Because I don't feel gay. I don't feel like those fags I see on television. I don't act like that. I'm a man. I'm just a man who loves sex. I'm a man who loves sex with women and I also happen to love sex with men. I'm just a man."

"Do you still love sex with women or is that something you do to make yourself feel like more of a man?"

Dorian paused. It was a question he had never asked himself. He thought he loved sex with women. But maybe he loved the chase, the different scent, and how it looked to the world more than the actual sex.

"Yeah, of course I do," Dorian said. "A hole is a hole."

Dorian tried to make light of it. At the same time, he didn't want to appear vulnerable to Justin, who never seemed to have a problem putting it all out there. Dorian still wanted to keep up appearances. He was actually scared by what he might be feeling for this man. He had never before allowed himself to have a relationship—not a deep one, at least—with anyone. Now he was sitting here feeling something for a man.

Justin, for his part, wasn't amused by the "a hole is a hole" comment.

"You know I'm kidding," Dorian said, trying to clean it up. "I'm just saying I enjoy sex—whether it's with a man or a woman. It's sex. It's an expression."

"I am going to tell you the truth," said Justin, who was finding little comfort in Dorian's comments. "After the other night, I can't imagine ever really enjoying sex with a woman again. I mean, I can do it. But what I experienced the other night was something that changed my life forever."

"Glad to have obliged," Dorian said, leaning in to kiss Justin. There was a reason Dorian didn't talk much. He knew his words usually got him in trouble. So he relied on the one thing that always seemed to work for him as he straddled Justin and kissed him passionately.

Justin, still a little stung by Dorian's cavalier attitude, couldn't resist the soft lips and gentle, probing tongue that became more ferocious as Justin responded. He found himself in that space again of complete and utter reckless abandon. He couldn't control anything as long as Dorian had his hands on his body. And Justin didn't want to be in control.

He had come to Dorian's looking for answers, and Justin had found the answers. In every stroke of his penis, in every lick of his balls, in every drop of come that shot out of him into Dorian's mouth, Justin found his answers.

But when he left there on this night, he still had one question.

What am I going to tell Tasha?

Chapter Eighteen

Anne sat in Columbus Circle enjoying the sunshine and the latest issue of *W*. A man was walking a Great Dane and she thought about how regal it was. Despite its enormous size, that dog had such a playful, fun energy. She began to daydream about owning one. Anne thought she would name hers Pluto; how great it would be to have a friend like that. She felt her phone vibrate in her pocket.

"Hello, this is Anne."

"Hey, Anne. I have some great news! Are you free this evening?" said Tasha.

The two hadn't really spent time together since that night. Tasha couldn't avoid Anne forever. She needed her for her business. Tasha wanted to catch up to make sure that what had happened between them was completely over and that it was something they could move past. There was a brief moment of silence on the phone after Anne said she was free and Tasha blurted out, "Because I have to."

"What did you say?" Anne asked. "You have to what?"

"Oh, nothing," Tasha said. "I must have had a Tourette's moment."

Tasha had been thinking out loud. Sloppy. She wished that she had been drinking the night she and Anne made love—it would have been just the excuse she needed. She was thinking about how she had to make it all right—for Anne, for her business, and for Justin. She had to put those pieces back together because she had to.

"So I'll pick you up at your place in a couple of hours, if that works for you," Tasha said.

"Yeah, sure. That sounds great," Anne said.

Anne put her thin phone into her coat pocket and began walking back toward her building. She continued to play back the words that had slipped from Tasha's mind and out into the universe.

Because I have to . . .

Anne knew that there was something behind that phrase and she couldn't let it go.

Because I have to . . .

What? Have me all to yourself?

Anne smiled at her wishful thinking and went to get ready for her night out.

Tasha wrote out Anne's check. She included a nice bonus. Anne had done a wonderful job on Justin's portfolio. And the model catalog that Anne had created had given Tasha more business than she could handle. She was actually overbooked and wanted to reward Anne. Tasha put the check for twenty-five thousand into an envelope and slipped it into her Louis bag.

She called Justin and told him that she had some business to take care of and not to wait for her for dinner. Tasha checked herself one more time in the full-length mirror, walked by the couch and the rug, had a brief flashback, pulled it together, and headed out to pick up Anne. She called downstairs for the Mercedes two-seater. She wanted to take Anne to this hot restaurant in Jersey, Voro, and the two-seater was a much smoother ride than the SUV.

Tasha was driven so much that she enjoyed driving every now and then, especially when there was potential for discomfort. She could get lost in the road and the music and not really have to focus on any conversation.

Tasha pulled in front of Anne's building and summoned the doorman. She didn't want to park legally, or get out of her car.

"I'll let Ms. Becker know that you're here," he said, going into the building to ring her. After a few minutes he came back out. "Ms. Becker will be down shortly."

Anne walked out, casually elegant in Gucci loafers, fitted jeans, and a white cashmere coat that stopped at her thighs.

The doorman began to follow Anne so he could open the door for her on the passenger side.

"No, please, Marvin," she said. "I'm fine. Thank you so much."

"Have a wonderful evening, Ms. Becker."

"You do the same," she said.

Anne had butterflies in her stomach as she started to get into the car. She got in and smiled at Tasha and leaned over for a peck on the cheek. It was awkward. And at the same time very welcome.

"So where are we headed?" said Anne, happy that the butterflies were flitting away and she was finally beginning to relax.

"Voro," she said. "It's in Jersey."

"That's a long way to go to eat," Anne laughed. "The food must be awesome."

"It is," Tasha said. "I wanted to be away from the city."

The truth was, Tasha was nervous about being seen with Anne. And she was known just about everywhere, thanks to the nosy-ass gossip pages and paparazzi. There were already dozens of "sightings" of Tasha and Justin showing up on Page Six and online, which she didn't mind. The intrigue over whether Tasha was bedding her hottest model actually got Justin more jobs. But she wasn't sure if she could contain her emotions while sitting across the table from Anne. One photo might tell a story Tasha never wanted told.

Voro was off the beaten track, had wonderful food and one of the best chocolate-fondue desserts she had ever had. The lighting was low and intimate, and the atmosphere was just what Tasha needed to say the things she wanted to say to Anne.

Tasha zipped across town, allowing her AMG engine to flex its muscles as she hit the Lincoln Tunnel and exit 15W on the turnpike to 280 West and was at the restaurant in less than thirty-five minutes.

"I would hate to see you on the autobahn!" said Anne. "I'm glad the top wasn't down. I know I would have lost some of my hair."

The two cracked up laughing. It was a break they both needed, as most of the ride had been filled with small talk and silence.

When they arrived at Voro, Anne was pleasantly surprised. It looked like something she would see in South Beach, Miami, with its torch lighting outside, and rich, dark-wood accents and floors, and trendy people inside.

Tasha checked their coats and headed up the stairs, reaching back for Anne's hand as she led her up the small, cavernous stairway to a private loft area that overlooked the dining area and entrance. Toward the back of the loft, which had four exclusive tables and a private bar, were two exquisitely made beds, with crisp white sheets. She couldn't help but notice the irony of it all.

"I love the mood of this place," Anne said, being a little fresh. "Where did you hear about it?"

"Well, my attorney, David, owns this place," she said. "I actually was here before he renovated. But this is my first time here since the renovation was finished."

Anne didn't bother to comment but wanted to. It was too easy to knock that softball out of the park. But Anne decided to not even swing.

"You look fabulous, Tasha," she said.

"Thanks, so do you," Tasha said. "But you always do."

Breaking up their mutual admiration society, the waitress came to the table to take their order.

"What can I get for you ladies?"

"You know, we have never been here before, so I think we will have one of everything on the appetizer menu," said Anne. "Is that okay with you, Tasha?"

"Of course," she said nervously. Tasha loved to eat but knew she had to watch it; she thought that she could probably get away with splurging for one night. She just wouldn't eat for the next three.

"Yeah, and let's get a bottle of your finest champagne," Tasha said. "We're celebrating."

Tasha slid an envelope across the table to Anne.

"This is for you," she said. "I want to say thank you for all of your help."

"You are very welcome, my friend," Anne said without opening it. "It was business. But it was also my *pleasure.*"

The two laughed at the joke between them as the food started coming to the table—grilled baby lollipop lamb chops, garlic shrimp, pan-seared crab cakes, plantain chips. Filet mignon slices grilled with Gorgonzola cheese, on a toasted baguette.

"We don't need an entrée, do we?" Tasha pleaded as she plowed into the food.

"No," Anne said. "But I do want dessert. Let's get that fondue you were talking about."

The fondue came, a spectacle unto itself. This elegant fountain of rich, dark chocolate surrounded by fresh strawberries, apples, bananas, and melon. There were metal sticks to jab the fruit with and let the chocolate fountain pour over it.

"Try this," Anne said, dipping a piece of banana into the chocolate stream.

Tasha took the piece into her mouth and closed her eyes.

"Oh my God. This is sinful!" said Tasha as Anne captured some of the excess chocolate dripping off Tasha's mouth with her index finger, licking it off.

It was a bold, erotic act that both excited Tasha and made her pull back. She was not going to go there with Anne. She could not. She must not. She nervously picked up her glass of champagne and offered a toast.

"To continued success," she said as they tapped glasses.

They both took a sip of the smooth Dom Pérignon and pretended not to be incredibly attracted to each other—fueled by the food, the chocolate, and the champagne.

"I saw the most beautiful dog today," Anne said. "It was a Great Dane, my favorite breed. It was so regal and lovable. They are so big, yet so graceful."

"Now what would you do with a dog that big, girl?" Tasha couldn't stop laughing. "That dog would wreck your place. And you travel so much, when would you have time to take care of him?"

"I would make time," Anne said. "I'm at a point in my career where I don't have to travel so much. I just do because I don't have anything to come home to."

Anne put down her glass to find Tasha looking right through her.

"Well, I like dogs, Anne," Tasha said, finding her serious voice. "I think that's great."

"So you understand what I mean when I talk about having someone to come home to," Anne said. "Is that what it is with Justin? Is he still staying with you?"

"Yeah, he's still staying with me," Tasha said, looking down at the table, trying not to make eye contact. "He's really great. I think that he might just be perfect for me."

Tasha threw back the last of her champagne and swallowed hard.

"Don't you mean he's no trouble?" Anne asked. "How can you think this pet project of yours is your perfect mate?"

Before Tasha could answer . . .

"I'll tell you why," said Anne, leaning in, forcing eye contact. "Because he is someone you think you created. Now he is in debt to you and you can control him. You want to control him whether you admit it or not. He is not on your level. I mean, what can the two of you possibly talk about?"

Anne got up from her seat and sat on the bench, right next to Tasha, who was still speechless.

"Yes, I know he's easy on the eyes," Anne continued. "So I guess he is perfect. You can show the world and every agency that turned you down how rich and successful you are and they can look at the beautiful man-child you have on your arm!"

Tasha felt herself choking up.

"That is not real, though, Tasha!" she said. "That's not real at all. How long have we been friends? I know you. I know you better than you know yourself. I know you inside and out. I know the places you haven't even allowed yourself to know. And what I know is that *he* is not perfect for you.

"I watched you achieve everything you went after. And I also watched the loneliness and the unhappiness. We have lived in parallel universes, because as I watched you, I lived it, too. And now you're telling me you have found your perfect match. I will agree with that, but it's not Justin!"

Tasha couldn't hold back the tears.

"So you think that I *want* to choose him over you?" Tasha pleaded. "I see you. You are the most beautiful person I know, in every way. But then what? Where do we go from here? Where do we go, Anne?!"

Tasha wiped her eyes with the back's of her hands and poured the rest of the bottle into her glass.

"I know it's you who would make it great for me, Tasha. Don't you feel it?"

"Yes, I do." Tasha slid close to Anne, pushing her easily along the varnished bench until they were completely in the corner and out of sight. "I love your mind and I love your body."

"Well, if you know—" Anne didn't get to finish her sentence.

Tasha couldn't help the overwhelming feeling that she had to kiss Anne. And before she realized it, she had leaned in for a kiss that seemed to last forever.

Anne stopped Tasha because she wasn't able to catch her breath and heard people coming.

"I'm ready to go," said Anne, who pulled out two crisp hundred-dollar bills and put them on the table. She helped her friend to her feet and got their coats.

Anne looked through Tasha's purse until she found the keys. She was in no condition to drive. Tasha slid onto the front seat and Anne started the car and buckled Tasha in.

"I *do* care about what people think, Anne," Tasha said. "I can't do this. Not now. And I can't change that. I'm not strong like you. I can't take not being perfect—or at least not appearing that way."

Those were the last words out of Tasha's mouth that evening.

A*nne called ahead* to Tasha's apartment so that Justin could come downstairs and help get her inside.

"Hey, Justin, I'm downstairs," she said. "Let her know that I'll call her in the morning."

Anne gave the parking attendant the keys to park the car and thought about hailing a cab. But she decided that she would walk home.

It was a long walk, but Anne needed the air. She needed to walk through the park.

Chapter Nineteen

Anne loved Central Park, and she often went there when she needed to cool off or think. It was one of those rare clear New York City nights, where the stars were visible and the moon seemed so close that you could almost touch it. It was bright and huge in the sky. Anne was lost in her thoughts.

"Why do I have to come second to him just because he's a man?" Anne muttered aloud, to herself. "Why am I still living for other people? How can she be so stupid?

"Anne," she said to herself. "You will continue to be a friend and you will be there to pick up the pieces."

She was walking briskly, her hands shoved deep into the pockets of her full-length white cashmere coat. She had her thick hair out, allowing it to breathe in the brisk air as the winter was straining to turn to spring. The days were in the midfifties, but the nights flirted with the forties. It was one in the morning and there were very few people roaming around the city that never sleeps. Central Park was one Anne's favorite places in the city. It was 843 acres of wonderment, big enough to have its very own zoo and reservoir.

She remembered stories her mother had told her of seeing Diana Ross on the Great Lawn in 1983. Anne's mother had actually braved the storm that canceled the first day's show and returned the next day to see the fabulous Miss Ross give what she called the most incredible performance she had ever seen. Anne's mother had pictures to prove it. After the concert, Anne's mother played Diana Ross records in their house so much that Anne became a de facto fan herself.

A few decades later, Anne got to experience the majesty of the Great Lawn as she stood with throngs of fans of the Dave Matthews Band. Their 2003 free concert was a thrill.

Anne would run through this park at least three times a week, from the spring until late fall. She Rollerbladed and biked in the summertime. She knew parts of Central Park that most didn't know existed. There were so many hidden trails and enchanted forests. And at this early time of the morning, when there were so few people around, it didn't feel like New York at all. It felt like an exotic jungle.

Anne headed north, where she planned to exit the park and head home. She was looking forward to making herself an after-midnight, or later, snack of cheese and crackers and a cup of cinnamon-plum tea. She planned to catch up on some of the shows she'd TiVoed the previous week and then doze off with the TV on, as she did every night.

Anne had a busy day ahead. While she still hadn't shaken the whole Tasha episode from her thoughts, she was professional enough to let it go. There would be no more back and forth on the matter. Anne was done with it. She would go back to being a creative director and even a solid friend. She would pretend that what was between her and Tasha had never happened and she would be happy for Tasha and Justin. That was the only way. She would do it "because I have to."

Anne cut through a wooded area that had a trail. It was a shortcut she had used frequently during the daytime. Because of her familiarity with it, she wasn't as alert as she usually was. She was relaxed, too relaxed, because she didn't notice the dark figure just ahead of her, who initially seemed like he was walking but wasn't moving at all. Anne was too caught up in her own thoughts to notice the man brandishing a .45 from underneath a long coat. She didn't notice him until it was much too late.

As Anne passed him he came up behind her, grabbing her around the neck with the nose of his gun pressed hard into her temple.

"Make a sound and I will blow your fucking brains out," he growled in a low voice.

Anne could smell his putrid breath. He refused to allow her to turn around. The man, who was well over six feet tall and more than two hundred and ten pounds, walked Anne off the path backward, deep into the woods. They arrived at a thickly wooded area several dozen yards off the trail. He shoved Anne, face-first, into a huge tree that, with its thick, veiny bark, had to be more than a couple of hundred years old. Anne heard a crunching sound coming from the front of her face as her nose broke on impact. She squealed with pain, which was compounded as the man punched her on the side of her mouth with all his might.

"I told you not to make a fucking sound, bitch!" he growled again.

Anne tried to muffle her cries. She was completely petrified as new thoughts occupied her mind.

Why did I cut through the park? she thought. What was I thinking? It's Central Park! I know better. Is he going to kill me? Am I going to die out here? Oh God!

She felt a rough hand reach around the front of her jeans, undo the button and zipper, and in one move rip both the jeans and her Victoria's Secret silk panties down to her ankles. She clamped her legs together as tightly as she could, horrified as she realized what was coming. But her strength and all of the working out she did was no match for this man.

"Yes, just the way I like them—tall and fit," he said as he rammed his thick penis between her legs from behind, finding her spot.

The pain ripped through Anne, from between her legs to her head as he banged her repeatedly into the tree at a furious pace. He kept the nose of the gun to her head as he continued to violate her, daring her to struggle, daring her to fight back. Anne turned slightly when he lowered the gun. He was putting on a condom.

"Yeah, bitch! I ain't going to jail for a ho like you!" he said as he swung a single and swift backhand to her face.

Anne wanted to faint. She wished she could just black out, numb her entire being. But she absorbed every disgusting, humiliating, and painful thrust. He came inside her with one last angry thrust. She let out a yell.

"You dumb bitch!" he said, pounding her face with a blow after each and every word. "I told you to shut the fuck up!"

Anne fell to the ground, pants and panties still around her ankles, holding her face.

The last thing she remembered was the man kicking her.

She woke up hours later to licking.

"Max! Max!" the owner called out. A Labrador mix had discovered a bloody, unrecognizable woman curled up in the fetal position with her pants and panties still around her ankles.

Chapter Twenty

Justin took a chance and called Dorian from the house phone. Tasha was plastered from the night before and hadn't moved since Anne had dropped her off several hours earlier. From her condition, Justin knew that Tasha wouldn't be stirring anytime soon. She usually liked to be at the office by nine, but Justin knew that even if she could wake up in time, the likelihood of her being in shape to face the world, Tasha Reynolds-like—which meant perfection—was nil.

He closed the door to the study, which was becoming Justin's private place to be alone with his thoughts. He picked up the phone and dialed Dorian.

Dorian recognized the number and with a puzzled look answered.

"Hello?" he said hesitantly. He knew from the caller ID that it was Tasha's home number but he couldn't imagine why she'd be calling him from there. The only time she called her models from home was if there was a problem.

"It's me, Justin."

"What the fuck are you doing calling me from there?" said Dorian incredulously. "Have you lost your fucking mind?!"

"No. I mean, yes. I mean, maybe—maybe I have," Justin said. "It's fine. Tasha's asleep. But I have to talk to you. I tried you at home first. I was going to come over."

"Well, what is it? What's so damned important that it can't wait?"

"I have to tell her," Justin said.

"Oh, hell no, you don't!" Dorian said. "Why? What's wrong with you? You don't like your life, do you? You don't like the way you've been living—all of this success? You want to throw all of that shit away?"

"No," Justin said. "I just can't do this anymore. I can't keep lying like this. I can't do it."

Dorian was exasperated, frustrated, and scared. He wasn't so much worried about Justin throwing everything away as he was about Justin saying something to Tasha and messing up his career. What had started as a titillating little romp in the sack had grown into much more than Dorian had bargained for.

"Okay. Okay!" Dorian screamed. "You don't have to live a lie anymore. It's over between us. So you have *nothing* to tell."

"What?"

Dorian didn't get to hear Justin's response because he clicked

Hang Up on the menu bar of his cell. He didn't want to hear another word. Dorian was determined not to get caught out there. He hit Ignore the three times Tasha's number popped up on his caller ID.

He was through with it.

Chapter Twenty-one

Tasha woke up as the sun pierced her eyelids, sending a wave of pain throughout her skull. She was happy this morning to be alone with her thoughts and her bad hangover breath. She decided she wasn't going into the office today no matter what. Since she'd started the business, Tasha had never taken a day off. Even her vacations were working ones. But it had been a whirlwind week for Tasha and she needed one day to collect her thoughts. She was losing it and she needed to pull it all back together, and quickly.

"What the fuck?!" said Tasha, wincing as she tripped over Justin's running shoe, stubbing her big toe and sending yet another shock of pain to her head. "This shit is fucking annoying! I'm too old to be tripping over shit that doesn't belong to me."

Tasha walked gingerly toward the door of her bedroom and locked it. She wanted no part of the early morning clatter that either Justin or the maid might be responsible for. Tasha then went to her lavish master bathroom, which was bigger than some living rooms. It had a huge white marble soaking tub that could fit four.

At least twice a week, Tasha indulged in a bath, loaded with Aveda salts, which she kept in full supply. She didn't like bubble baths. They were too messy and not as relaxing as the salts, which left her skin as smooth as a baby's. Tasha had only really started using the tub when Justin moved in. He loved to take a bath, and it was a nice quiet time for them both to unwind. They might share a bottle of wine. The bath would invariably become part of their foreplay.

On this day, Tasha just wanted to get in the shower, turn it to steaming hot, and stand there until that water cleansed her—right down to her soul. She stood at the double vanity, squeezed out a dollop of her Origins Checks and Balances, and gently massaged her face, rubbing away the makeup from the previous night, paying extra attention to her pulsing temples. She put a thick rag under the water, rang it out, and just let it sit on her face for a minute, absorbing the warmth.

She tried to melt away the thoughts that seemed to cloud her mind.

Do I want to be responsible for Justin? Do I want to keep him around?

And what would I do with Anne? Can we just be a secret item?

Tasha leaned into the mirror, checking her teeth. She thought about how she was able to be more honest with herself with a hangover than she was without.

She stepped into the steamy shower thinking about how much of a coward she was.

"Yes, Tasha, you are a coward," she muttered to herself. "You're going to hold on to Justin even if you're not happy because it is in your nature to care what other people think."

Tasha bit her bottom lip with a raised eyebrow when she realized that not only was she talking out loud to herself, but she was also responding. She wondered if anyone else knew that she was certifiably crazy. She had created this imaginary world for herself years ago. And now she was actually living in it.

Tasha never took into account all the mental changes that occurred along the way—like how she was hurt by men more often than she cared to admit and that she was so open to the possibilities of being with a woman. Anne didn't happen by accident. Anne happened because Tasha wanted it to happen. And inside, Tasha also knew that she wanted it to keep happening. With a woman like Anne, Tasha could finally let her guard down completely and be entirely herself, and she liked how that felt. She had dabbled before with little flirtations, but this time she had gone too far. She'd never imagined she would fall so hard.

"I will have to go to the grave with this one," Tasha whispered to herself.

She wasn't going to think about it or speak about it again. She would never admit the truth to Justin. And after today, she wasn't going to ever admit it to herself again either.

"Justin, I'm choosing you," she said, stepping out of the shower, feeling a whole lot better than when she'd gone in. "I'm choosing you, baby."

Tasha grappled with whether she would speak to Anne face-to-face or just pretend that everything was okay and not even bring it up. But she knew that Anne wasn't going to let it go. So despite her cowardice, Tasha knew she had to talk to the lady and let her know what the deal was going to be. She braced herself as she picked up the phone in the bedroom. Her stomach jumped a bit as she dialed the number.

As she pressed the numbers, she could hear a voice already on the line.

"Hello?" she said.

"Tasha, it's me," said Justin, sounding very startled. "I'm on a call."

"Um, can you use your cell?" she said curtly. "I have to make an important call. Thanks!"

Without waiting for a response, Tasha slammed down the phone. She was annoyed that she had to wait even a second in her own house to use her own phone. Her moods were swinging faster than a Six Flags Air Racer.

Before she could pick it up again to dial Anne's number, there was a knock at the door.

What now? she thought.

"Tasha, open up." It was Justin. "I have to tell you something."

Tasha thought that maybe she had gone too far with her attitude. The last thing she wanted to do at this point was completely push him away. She did what she knew would erase any anger he might have toward her. She dropped her robe, walked toward the door, took a deep breath, and swung it open.

Before Justin could get a single word out, Tasha had her tongue in his mouth and was working her way into his briefs with her hand. He tried to pull her off him, but she wasn't having it as she guided him toward the bed and sat on top of him. He tried again to speak, but she placed her palm over his mouth and let her mouth find his penis.

With his last bit of strength, Justin spoke up.

"Tasha, stop!" he said, more emotional than she had ever seen him. "It's Anne. I was on the phone when another call came in. Anne was hurt last night. She's in the hospital!"

"The hospital? What the fuck happened?" Tasha said, and then she had a chilling thought. "Oh no! My car! She crashed my fucking car, didn't she?!"

"No, Tasha! She didn't crash your car." Justin's tone had a bite. He couldn't believe that Tasha's first thought was her precious car. "Your car is safe in the garage. When she dropped you off, she gave me the keys."

"Then what the fuck happened?!"

"I don't know," he said. "But it sounded pretty serious. I think we should get there and see about her."

"Yeah, yeah," Tasha said. "We have to go. But I can't be out in public looking like this. I need some time to get myself together."

Justin rolled his eyes.

"This isn't about you," he muttered under his breath.

"Excuse me?" Tasha said, whipping around before heading into the bathroom to put on her face. "*What* did you say?"

"Nothing," he said. "I'll be downstairs when you're ready."

Chapter Twenty-two

Anne lay in the narrow hospital bed, alone with her thoughts. Her left eye was swollen nearly shut and she could feel pain throughout her body—especially between her legs—despite whatever drugs they had her on. For one of the first times she could remember, Anne Becker was afraid.

She had never so much as had a spanking in her entire life. This rape had left her battered inside more than out.

First, she was subjected to all of the physical probing and the rape-kit procedures, which made her feel like she was getting raped all over again. The nurse who took the various tests started with an HIV lecture that sounded more as if it were coming from a drill sergeant than a supposedly compassionate healthcare provider.

After that, the nurse took her blood and put her clothes in a plastic bag to be examined by the police. Then Nurse Sampson took scissors and clipped about fifteen strands of Anne's hair. She was at least kind enough to take it from the middle of her head. But she didn't take as much care when she clipped a patch from Anne's pubic region, making her look like a bald chicken in one spot.

Jeez, can this get any worse? Anne thought.

It did. After that came the cotton swab under her nails, and the pelvic and vaginal exam. She even took a swab and swiped it around Anne's anal area. And then she left her with some literature on HIV and other sexually transmitted diseases as well as information on tetanus.

The physical exam was followed by the police probe. They sent in a female officer, thinking that was the more sensitive thing under the circumstances. But the woman cop, with her thick neck and gruff demeanor, was harder than any man. She asked the questions in a very impersonal, cold manner, forcing Anne to relive every horrific moment and detail. Anne wanted to forget the previous night—all of it. Even the time spent with Tasha, which was more of a tease than anything else. It only made her want something that she could never have, and that was torturous.

Just as she was about to spiral into a depression, her door swung open.

Anne threw the pamphlets in the drawer next to her bed.

"Oh my God! Are you okay, honey?" Darryl came swooshing into the room with all of the drama he could muster up—one of his hands over his mouth, tearing up and shaking all over, while his other hand clutched a beautiful bouquet of pink lilies.

Anne wanted to smile at the sight, but the split, swollen lip made it painful to stretch her mouth in that way. She loved Darryl for bringing her back a little bit of her life, but she could tell he was upset to see her in her current condition.

"Do I look *that* bad?" she mumbled.

"I was losing my mind on the way over here," said Darryl, purposely not answering her question. "I cannot believe this! I cannot believe this! Is there anything I can do to make you more comfortable?"

He leaned over and kissed her on the forehead—one of the areas not bandaged or swollen—and caressed her hand.

Before she could respond, Darryl was back in action.

"I need to check your calendar and cancel all of your appointments. Where is your phone?" Darryl said, scanning the room. "Well, it must be here somewhere. The call came from your phone. I was your ICE number."

Darryl had felt even closer to Anne when the police told him he was her "In Case of Emergency" contact.

"You know, you never think anything is going to happen," Darryl said. "At least I didn't until now. I don't even have an ICE number in my phone. But after this, I'm making sure I put you right there. I'm just glad I could be here for you."

"I'm glad you're here too, sweetie," Anne said, enduring the pain as a smile crossed her broken face. She felt her throat tightening and tears at the corners of her eyes because she knew Tasha was actually the *first* ICE number in her phone. Darryl was the second.

"You never know how important someone is in your life until something happens," Darryl said, finally breaking down the mask he wore so often that even he believed it was who he really was. "I really don't know what I would do without you. You are my best friend."

Anne didn't want to speak. The lump in her throat seemed the size of a grapefruit. She hadn't known how much she appreciated Darryl, either. He was not only there for her, he genuinely loved her. Anne was an only child, but in Darryl she felt as if she had a little brother.

"You know, I was raped," he said, out of the blue, cutting through the silence like a buzz saw. "Yep. I was ten years old . . . my uncle. It was real bad and I couldn't tell my mom. In fact, I never told a soul until now. I was too embarrassed. I knew it wasn't my fault, but I was still embarrassed and ashamed. I felt like a worthless piece of shit."

Tears flowed freely down Darryl's face as he sat at Anne's bedside. Tears stung her eyes. Most of their relationship revolved around the business, witty banter, and industry gossip. He would share his latest love with Anne and she would give him advice. She hadn't really gotten into the whole Tasha thing with him, but he knew. He knew her without words.

"I should have left her alone," Anne said.

"No. You had to follow your heart, baby. You had to see. But she's just not ready for all of this. You are too fierce and too complete for someone so shallow. Sometimes you need more than a connection."

"Yeah, I know. But I love her. I don't know why. I don't even want to. I just do."

"It's okay," Darryl said, dabbing tears from Anne's eyes with the tissue and taking a few out to dab his own eyes. "That love stuff is so confusing. That's why I just keep me a boy toy. It's less complicated, less painful. When we're done, we're done. *Hasta la vista.* I absolutely know that I'm missing out on something. But I'm willing to miss out on it. I really am."

"You know I was content to be by myself. I wasn't looking for this."

"I know, I know," he said. "So what are you going to do? How do you feel about her now?"

"I love her. And I hate her. I mean, there's a part of me that blames her for my being here. I mean, what in the world was I thinking, walking through Central Park at that time of night, by myself? I had to be out of my flipping mind! I hate to say this, D, but I want her to feel some of this."

"Oh, she will," Darryl assured her. "Karma is a bitch on her period. She is not to be fucked with."

"I don't want her physically hurt, I just want her to wake up and not be so shallow and live a truthful life."

"Truthful? You want her to not be shallow? What industry do we work in? Hey . . . I got an idea to teach Miss Tasha a lesson."

Anne perked up. Darryl was always good for hatching a plan, and it kept her mind off her pain—that and the button releasing morphine into her IV when the pain got to be too much. The broken bones, the vaginal shredding, the ruptured bladder, that would all heal. But what she was feeling inside was going to take a little longer.

"Why don't we show Tasha what's *really* important," Darryl said. "By taking away something that she thinks is hers."

She looked at him, puzzled.

"That Jamaican masterpiece," Darryl said. "He's the center of her world. She has put so much into him. Let's see what will happen if he's no longer there. And not just him. I have a lead on a couple of other models with the Tasha Reynolds Agency that I can get to, and so can you."

"Okay, I see where you're going," Anne said. "But how can we pull this off?"

"You leave all of the details to me. I got this. I got you. Miss Tasha will be getting the wake-up call of her life!"

One hour later

"I told you that you didn't have to come with me," Tasha said through clenched teeth as they hustled through the sterile halls of the hospital, heading to Anne's room.

"You were in no condition to do this alone," Justin said. "Besides, I want to be there for Anne, too. She's done a lot for me and I want her to know that I'm here for her."

The conversation ended abruptly at the doorway of Anne's room. The sight of Anne left them both speechless. The wonderful cheekbones that set off her face were so swollen that her face looked bloated and unrecognizable. The cheekbones looked like they were straining to break through the skin. Both eyes had huge, puffy bruises underneath; the left was nearly closed shut. She had a bandage on her mouth, hiding her hideously split lip.

"Wha-what happened?" Tasha said, breaking the thick silence.

"I guess I was in the wrong place at the wrong time," said Anne, trying to make light of it and at the same time trying to stem the fury that was building.

"No, really. What happened? I don't remember much of last night, but I do know that you dropped me off," Tasha said.

Anne couldn't look at her. And she didn't want to speak. So she lay there, staring down at the crisp white linens on her twin-size hospital bed. Then she looked at Tasha and Justin standing together.

"Justin, sweetie, I need to talk to Anne alone," Tasha said in the nicest tone she could muster up. "Thanks for coming, but I'd like some time alone with her."

"Okay, no problem," Justin said, walking over to Anne's bed and giving her a gentle kiss on her swollen cheek.

"If you need anything, I'm here for you," he said to Anne, who gave his hand a squeeze.

He gave Tasha a peck, too, as he left the room. Once outside the hospital, Justin made another attempt to call Dorian. There was no answer. He wanted to slam the phone onto the concrete. He wanted to punch something. Instead, he pulled himself together and went for a walk. He ran into Darryl, who was heading back.

I can't believe my good fortune, Darryl said to himself. I was wondering how I would get that hunk of a man without that vampiress! This is going better than I expected.

"Justin!" Darryl called out, startling Justin, who wasn't expecting anyone here to know him.

"Hey, Darryl," Justin said. "I'm so sorry about what happened to Anne. What did happen, exactly?"

"She didn't tell you?" he asked.

"No, and I understand if it's personal," Justin said. "I just . . . I just really like her and . . . is there anything I can do?"

"No, well . . . there is something you can do," Darryl said, seizing the opportunity. "There is something you can do that would make Anne feel a whole lot better."

"What is it? I'll do it!"

"Leave Tasha," Darryl said.

"What? Are you crazy?! Why would I want to do that?"

"When you hear what I'm about to tell you, there is no way you will stay."

And so their plan was hatched.

Chapter Twenty-three

Back in the hospital room

"So you're not going to talk to me?" Tasha stood over Anne, her arms folded.

"What do you want me to say?" Anne said.

"Say something," Tasha said. "You can start by telling me what happened and how you ended up here."

"That I don't want to talk about," Anne said. "Let's just say I got some sense knocked into me."

"What is that supposed to mean?"

"I know what I need to do now," Anne said. "I know I need to leave you alone."

Tasha was stung. While she was definitely going to put Anne out of her life—at least personally—she never expected "the breakup" to come from Anne. Tasha didn't like it. She wanted to be the one to make that decision and she wasn't 100 percent sure now that she wanted it to *be* over.

"You can't leave me alone," Tasha said, cockily. "I'm too much in you. You can't just walk away from all of this."

"I can and I will," said Anne. "Because I must. You're toxic. And you're killing me slowly."

"Oh, hell no! You're not blaming me for you being in the hospital?" Tasha asked. "I know you're not doing that, are you?"

"No, I'm blaming myself for allowing you to occupy so much of my thoughts," Anne said. "I'm blaming myself for allowing you to distract me at the wrong times, for not having good judgment, for not being myself."

"I didn't *force* you to do anything," Tasha said. "As I remember it, *you* came on to me! You started all of this."

"I started it and I'm ending it," Anne said. "But it's not just about this thing we had between us. It's about you and your attitude, your sense of entitlement, your shallow nature. I can't understand what I ever found attractive about you."

"Oh please! Miss me-with-all-of-that-self-righteous-bullshit Anne," Tasha shot back. "You know *exactly* what you found attractive. It's the very thing you *still* find attractive."

Anne was angry now. She was angry because Tasha was right. There was still something pulling her. There was still something about this woman Anne had a hard time shaking.

Anne's bottom lip quivered as she tried to form a word, any word. She was having a hard time finding words as tears betrayed her. She was also having a hard time *not* crying. It was as if someone had loosened a faucet somewhere and Anne couldn't seem to shut it off.

For as long as Tasha had known Anne, she had never seen her cry, or even lose her temper. She was always on an even keel and totally prepared to handle any situation.

"I was raped last night," Anne said matter-of-factly, collecting herself and completely catching Tasha off guard.

"What? How? When?" Tasha fired back. Her mind was reeling.

"It happened after I dropped you off . . ."

Anne told her story slowly and Tasha listened intently. By the time Anne was done, they were both crying.

"I am so sorry that happened to you," said Tasha, breaking an uncomfortably long silence. "I am so sorry."

"Me, too," Anne said. Her statement was loaded and Tasha picked up on it.

"I didn't mean for any of this to happen," Tasha said. "I didn't plan to fall in love with you."

"Love?" Anne queried incredulously.

"Yes, love."

"Do you even know what that word means? What does it mean to *you,* Tasha? I mean really. Are you leaving Justin?"

"No," said Tasha, reluctantly. "You know I can't do that."

"I know that you *won't* do that!" Anne said. "I know that you are far too selfish and self-absorbed to do anything that might hurt your image or your business. You cannot see beyond your own ego. None is so blind than those who cannot see."

"I'm going to let all of that slide because I know you're hurting," Tasha shot back. "But just know that I am far from selfish. Not being with you is the most selfless thing I can do. You don't know what you're talking about."

"I know one thing," Anne said.

"What's that?"

"I know that the wonderful Jamaican who left this room is not happy, either," Anne said. "So you're making all of these decisions and nobody's happy."

"Oh, *he's* happy!" Tasha was getting defensive. "He has everything any man could want—including me. Again, Anne, you don't know what you're talking about. Get some rest, sweetie. Get some rest. I'll be back tomorrow."

"Don't bother," Anne said. "Darryl will be here to take me home. And I won't be doing any work for you."

"I don't expect you to do anything for a while. Take as long as you need."

"I may need forever," Anne said.

"Now you're going too far," said Tasha. "Let's have this discussion when you're not drugged up, when you're feeling better."

Tasha's business hadn't officially taken off until Anne Becker lent her magic touch to the portfolios, photo shoots, and direction. Anne was as important to Tasha's success as Tasha was herself. She didn't want to lose Anne's expertise. But deep down inside, Tasha didn't want to lose her friendship, and more.

"Hey, I'm sorry for hurting you," Tasha said.

"You're only sorry about what you are going to lose," said Anne. "I doubt if you're truly remorseful."

"How can you say that!" said Tasha, showing the most hurt look she could muster up. "I *never* wanted to hurt you."

Anne stared at Tasha through swollen, cold eyes, unmoved.

"Like I said, we should talk about this when you get out and have had some time to think," said Tasha. "If you need anything in the time being, I'm here for you. I know you don't think so, but I am."

Tasha leaned over and kissed Anne on the cheek. Anne didn't move. Tasha turned and left. One tear ran down the right side of Anne's face.

Chapter Twenty-four

Anne returned to her home to find flowers everywhere. Her place looked and smelled like an expensive florist's, and it made her smile.

"Darryl," she said to herself.

Her longtime friend had become even closer to her since her stay in the hospital. He was helping her heal inside and out, and she was allowing him. Anne liked depending on someone for once in her life. She prided herself on being independent and self-sufficient. She'd left Germany when she was just seventeen. She found success relatively quickly because of her beauty, but more so because of her brains. As an only child, she was used to getting her way. But her German father was a strict disciplinarian who instilled in his daughter not just a sense of purpose, but also a sense of order. She understood at an early age that there was a formula to every outcome. You just had to know beforehand what that formula was and what outcome you wanted. Anne was a careful planner.

Even her move to the United States had been planned for years. While her parents thought their obedient little girl was going to study physics at the university and be either a doctor or a professor, Anne had other plans. She was going to explore her creative side in America. She didn't tell her plan to anyone; she just mapped it out carefully, putting all of the elements into play to ensure success. Then she made her move. Her parents were mad as hell, but they also knew that with Anne's determination, there was no way to stop her. They knew she would not be returning, that she was going to accomplish everything she set out to accomplish. Anne never lost.

Now she had a teammate, a partner in crime, in Darryl. While Anne was never big on revenge, she was big on making things right. Tasha wasn't right. It wasn't right that Tasha didn't choose her—not because Anne wanted Tasha but because she knew that Tasha really wanted to be with Anne. It wasn't right how Tasha was using Justin . . . and using Anne . . . and using everyone around her.

Sure, it would be a whole lot easier just to walk away. But what fun would that be? And more important, it would be like leaving an animal with rabies loose to strike again.

"She needs to be taught a lesson, that one," Anne said to no one in particular. Darryl called to make sure she was okay and to see if she needed anything.

"Why aren't you here already?" Anne asked.

"I wanted to give you your space," said Darryl, who had a

key to her place. "I wanted you to get comfortable and get back to normal. But I'll be over in a few."

After hanging up from Darryl, she got a buzz from downstairs.

"Now, who could that be?" Anne said as she walked over to the intercom.

"Yes?"

"Miss Becker, you have, um, an unusual delivery," her doorman said.

"Well, what is it?"

"I think I should just bring it up and let you see for yourself," he said.

"Okay, Phillip. Bring it up."

Anne waited by the door as Phillip exited from the elevator.

"What the . . . ," was all Anne could say.

In a huge basket was a harlequin Great Dane puppy. It looked like a full-grown dalmatian.

"This was something I didn't want to tell you about, I had to show you, Miss Becker," Phillip said apologetically.

"I see. Thank you, Phillip," said Anne, attempting to grab the heavy basket.

"Let me help you with that," Phillip said, heading into her doorway with the basket.

"No, that's okay." Anne was very suspicious now, even of Phillip, who had been her doorman for the last four years. "I will manage. Thank you."

She handed him a twenty-dollar bill that she had in the pocket of her Polo pajama bottoms.

The basket was heavy and she was far from healed. She put it down on the plush carpet. She took the card that was buried in the black-and-white blanket wrapped around the matching dog.

Please accept this gift as a token of my love and appreciation. I think he will help you recuperate. I wish I could. Please forgive me—Tasha.

"That damned woman!" Anne said. "Why can't she just play fair? I can't accept this dog!"

But when she bent down and looked into the very human eyes of this dog, her heart melted. There was an instant connection as he wriggled free from the basket and the blanket and bounded around her apartment as if he belonged there.

"Wait! Wait!" Anne said. She was in no condition to chase a dog around her house. At the sound of Anne's voice, the dog stopped in its tracks and came to her.

"Oh, you're a smart one," she said, bending down very slowly to rub behind his ears. His clipped tail wagged furiously and he sat down. Anne smiled.

"I will call you Maximillian—a big name for a big dog," Anne whispered. "Max."

The dog started jumping up on her.

"No!" she said. And he stopped. Although he was a puppy, he was still very big and would only get bigger. Great Danes were known to grow to well over six feet (standing on their hind legs) and weigh more than a hundred and fifty pounds. The one she'd seen that day in the park was regal and beautiful, but huge. She really looked at Max and saw that he was even more regal and even more beautiful than that dog. But based on the size of his paws, he was going to be huge, too.

Oh, brother! This is going to be work, she thought.

Anne smiled at the thought, though. She loved to work.

Darryl arrived as planned, puzzled by the dog running through Anne's place like a little black-and-white version of Marmaduke.

"What the fuck is this?" he said.

"Oh, it's a gift from Tasha."

"Okay, so when are you sending it back?"

"I'm not," Anne said. "I'm keeping him."

"What?!"

"Yes. I'm keeping him. His name is Maximillian. But you can call him Max."

"Have you lost your mind?" Darryl said. "When do you have time to take care of a dog? And do you know how big this thing is going to get? I've seen them the size of horses. I mean, who's going to walk this beast and pick up his king-size shit? You? I can't see it."

"I couldn't see a lot of things," Anne said. "But I'll figure it out."

"Please don't tell me that you're going soft on me," Darryl said, the back of his hand on his forehead, looking like he was going to faint. "Please don't tell me that all of my hard work will be for naught. Are you buying this bitch's bullshit? You just can't. Not with all of the work I've done!"

"D, baby, don't fret," Anne said. "Just because I've fallen in love with another man doesn't mean that I have lost my fangs. Please, update me."

Anne sat gingerly on her couch, with Max, her new love, next to her, resting his big head in her lap. The act of petting him was both comforting and pleasing.

"So tell me everything," Anne said. "What came of your conversation with Justin?"

Chapter Twenty-five

After his conversation with Darryl, Justin was just one big ball of confusion, a raw nerve. He didn't know whether he was coming or going. He'd just found out that Tasha had been cheating on him, that his whole life with her was some big game, some showboat to solidify Tasha's place as the grande dame of the modeling world. He had fallen for her, really fallen for her, and now he was very confused. He was angry and hurt. But his feelings were complicated because of everything that had happened between him and Dorian. He'd been contemplating leaving, even before all of this. But now he knew he had to.

He was also confused about something for the first time in his life—his sexuality. The past few months with Dorian had thrown all of that into the balance. It had started in London and had grown into a raging fire—burning away his desire for Tasha and any other woman. With Dorian, Justin felt complete for the first time in his life.

The funny thing was that he hadn't known something was missing in his life until then. It was like when he tasted Junior's cheesecake for the first time. After that, when he thought of cheesecake, that's what he would think about. He could enjoy another brand, but Junior's, with its amaretto and graham cracker crust and its juicy, ripe strawberries, completely satisfied his palate.

Dorian had awakened something inside Justin that might have been dormant all along. Or perhaps he'd created something new inside him. Whatever the case, Justin was now clear that what he wanted, what he craved, was the touch, the smell, the feel of a man.

He didn't just want cheesecake. He wanted Junior's.

So, Darryl's little proposition, while a surprise, wasn't a stretch. He had to leave Tasha. But the question was, how? What would he say to her? How could he tell her? He had no one to talk to. Tasha kept him completely isolated. He hadn't made any friends outside of Dorian. And now he couldn't talk to him either.

Dorian wasn't answering his phone.

Tasha was at the office, as usual.

How could she just go back to business as usual, with everything that was going on? Maybe she really is some sort of Ice Queen who can put a nice face on anything. What a phony.

Justin had so much on his mind. He was resigned that he would never again be with Dorian. If Justin had one thing, it was pride. Pride had made him say one more word to his father, who had threatened not to buy him a motorbike for his fourteenth birthday if he said another word. He said another word, defiantly.

"Boy, you keep cutting off your nose to spite your face," his ma-ma would say to him. "You are some kind of stubborn."

But for Justin, it was a matter of principle. That was big for him. He didn't care what he lost in the process. And Justin had also learned never to chase anything. He eventually got the motorbike and even a car for graduation. So he wasn't going to chase Dorian.

"He'll be back," Justin said assuredly.

In the meantime, though, Justin was messed up. His emotions were raw and frayed. He felt guilty for how he had cheated on Tasha. He also felt betrayed by Tasha. He was completely hurt by Dorian. He wanted to run away. He wished he could just go to JFK, hop on a plane, and go home. He wished he could forget, just rewind the last few years of his life and be back on that farm, chopping cane. Things had been so simple then.

Justin walked the streets of New York aimlessly. He must have traversed more than thirty city blocks. As he neared Hell's Kitchen, a sign across the street caught his eye. He had passed this place more than a hundred times, but he'd never noticed it until now.

ARCADE

Fun and games was the first thing that came to mind. Justin was never one for games. Not even as a kid. When most were playing hide-and-seek outside or in the courtyard of his school, Justin preferred to be inside on the computer perfecting his chess game. He was always a bit of loner and just a little different. When he got into his teens, while others were hanging out in video game places or battling one another on Game Boys or PlayStations at each other's houses, Justin wasn't. He didn't much care for those mind-numbing games.

But this arcade had a strange pull. He checked his watch. It was three thirty. Tasha would not be home until after five. He had plenty of time to check out this place and still be home in time to prepare her a scrumptious meal and draw her bath. She had him on a schedule. What had started out as something Justin did to show his gratitude and love had become expectation. He was a glorified manservant.

But right now, he was feeling as if he wanted to do something out of his routine—try something off the beaten path. He was looking for an escape. Stepping into the doorway of the arcade, Justin knew he was about to do something entirely new to him.

There was an ominous-looking figure at the door, a man about six feet four and very beefy. He didn't speak. He just pointed Justin inside. Justin adjusted his baseball cap, pulling it way down, practically covering his eyes. He didn't want to be recognized. His face had graced the covers of magazines in three countries; this was one place he didn't want to be spotted.

There was a menu on the wall for live shows, with times. There was a twenty-dollar cover to get into the live shows—featuring strippers, lap dances, and revues—that played on the half hour. The lighting was very bad, so Justin had to squint to see all of the items.

Instead of paying for anything, Justin decided to just observe.

There was a staircase leading down. The walls were painted a dirty red. While upstairs was the live action, downstairs was the *real* live action. At the bottom of the stairs was a hallway that had five doors on either side. Behind each door was a small room, where for twenty-five cents there would be a three-minute video of your choice. Two men and a woman, anal, oral—whatever your pleasure. A coin machine that dispensed quarters was at the end of the hall, as well as a magazine rack filled with every kind of XXX magazine imaginable.

Justin checked his pocket. He had fifty cents. He decided to check out one of the rooms. His adrenaline was flowing. He was scared and excited all at at the same time.

"What the fuck am I doing?" he asked himself. But there was no response. He swallowed hard and opened the first door. There was someone inside.

"Excuse me," Justin said, nervously, as he gently began to close the door.

"No, no problem at all," said the figure he could barely see inside the darkness. "Come in."

Justin hesitated but then went in. The smell was pungent—a mix of sweat and funk and sex—an unmistakable scent. The man was two minutes into his film, which was viewed on a twenty-five-inch screen. There was one plush velvet movie-theater-style seat in front of the screen. There wasn't really room for much else. Justin pulled the door closed and stood behind the chair. The man offered Justin the chair. He had decided to abandon his flick for a live show. As Justin was watching the two men on the screen—one with a huge erection, the other giving him the best blow job Justin had ever seen—Justin was about to get one of his own.

The stranger kneeled between Justin's legs and teased him, unzipping his loose-fitting jeans. He pulled up Justin's T-shirt, revealing his eight-pack abs. Mr. Stranger balanced himself on the arms of the chair and balanced his own hard body over Justin's. He went to work on Justin's abs and quickly moved to the bulging, pulsing hard-on trapped, like a giant curled-up python, inside his jeans, beneath the end of the zipper. Justin was commando. He loved wearing no underwear. He loved the way his dick felt against the soft cotton of his jeans. But now it was getting uncomfortable as he was getting more and more aroused.

Mr. Stranger was a mind reader. He was like a surgeon, extracting Justin's thick, heavy manhood without pulling down his pants. It was an art, keeping the bottom part of the zipper from snagging Justin's hair or balls.

The man managed to get Justin's whole meat into his mouth, forcing a surprising moan from Justin. It was the only sound made between the two. Justin thought he would explode right in this stranger's mouth. The thrill of this forbidden encounter, coupled with the actual sensation, was too much.

Justin took a deep breath. Or tried to. Because Mr. Stranger went to work like a hungry wolf, tearing Justin's meat up with the right amount of force, and the perfect amount of wetness and softness. It was as if this man was inside his dick, knowing every single itch that needed to be scratched. The movie clicked off, and two minutes later, Justin busted off, grabbing a handful of the man's dark curly hair. It seemed to excite the man even more as Mr. Stranger moaned, lapping up every drop of come and gently milking what was left. Justin had to push him off to make him stop.

He thought he would just keep coming if Mr. Stranger didn't stop. He was losing it. Justin quickly got up, zipped up his pants, and left.

His legs were weak and he couldn't quite feel the ground under him. He just kept walking. He walked right out of there. He hailed a cab when he got outside. He didn't think he could make it home without collapsing. He had to catch his breath and collect himself.

The twelve blocks to the loft seemed like a drive to the Hamptons. Justin spent the ride with his head in his hands. His head was swirling.

"What the fuck did I just do?" he said aloud.

Justin was ashamed. He vowed never to go back. He made it home and jumped in the shower, as hot as he could stand it. He tried to wash off the thought of what had just happened. He tried to wash away the thought of Dorian, too. But as he thought about it, he got instantly hard. He squeezed some Paul Mitchell sage-and-lemon wash into his hands and started to stroke his member. As the water beat down on his back, cascading over his body, Justin jacked off with a fury, tugging and pulling and stroking and kneading. He ended up on his knees on the floor of the shower, completely spent for the second time that day.

Tasha would be home within the hour. He had to get dinner started.

Chapter Twenty-six

The long, hot shower washed away more than the seedy encounter. It washed away Justin's desire to keep up the charade. He toweled off, grabbed a gym bag, and threw some of his things into the bag, mostly everything he'd come with from Jamaica and some other items that meant something to him, collected over the last few years.

After he packed, he started dinner, as he had planned. Tasha was running late, which was a relief because Justin needed all of the time he could get to prepare himself for what he was about to do.

Justin was in his favorite room—the study—when Tasha sprang into their home, throwing her keys and bag on the table at the door. She was met by the aroma of brown-stew fish, rice-n-peas, cabbage and plantains, fried to perfection. She hadn't smelled that particular meal in some time. It was her favorite.

"To what do I owe this pleasure?" Tasha sang out, in search of Justin. "Why are you trying to spoil me? Where are you?"

Upon hearing her come in, he headed to the kitchen, where Tasha found him getting plates to set the table in the dining room.

"Hmmm, a romantic dinner, huh?" she said, wrapping her arms around his waist from the back as he lit the candles at the center of the table.

"I guess you can say that," he said. "Take those clothes off and get ready to eat."

"Are we talking food?" Tasha said, still holding him from behind, allowing one hand to slip around to caress his manhood.

"I'm talking food," Justin said, taking her hand from his member and kissing it. "Go on. I'll make your plate."

"Okay, easy on the plantains," she said. "You know I have to watch my figure. And so do you!"

Tasha and Justin ate without much conversation. Justin normally wasn't talkative, but he seemed extra quiet on this night.

"You don't say," Tasha finally said. "Is there something on your mind?"

Tasha wasn't sure she wanted to know. She was just about spent after that brief confrontation with Anne earlier.

"I can't do this," Justin whispered.

"What?!" Tasha said. "What did you say? I didn't hear you."

Justin cleared his throat. "I said, I can't do this."

"Can't do what?" Tasha was clueless.

"This. I can't be with you anymore."

"What?! What are you talking about?" She was completely puzzled.

"I can't keep living this lie," said Justin, never making eye contact. He couldn't bear to look into her eyes and see the hurt that must be there.

"So what was this? The last fucking supper?" Tasha said, grabbing his face from across the table, forcing him to look at her. "You must be out of your fucking mind! Is *everybody* losing their minds?"

"Actually, I haven't felt more sane in my entire life, Tasha. I don't want to upset you, but I have to be honest with you."

"You don't want to *upset* me?" said Tasha, her eyes darting wildly. "Well, it's too fucking late for that. I am *officially* upset. So you better have something better to say than, 'I can't do this anymore.' You better say something else because I'm trying not to hear that shit. Not after all I've done for you."

"Oh, there we go with that," Justin said. Now he was getting angry. "I am sick and fucking tired of you throwing that shit in my face! You act like you plucked some porch monkey out of the jungle and civilized him. I wasn't Tarzan when you met me. And I'm going to let you in on something else: *I was far from poor.*"

"Well, you weren't Justin Blakeman, world-renowned supermodel, face of everything, with a billboard in Times Square. I did that for you, you ungrateful fucking bastard!"

"Did I *ask* you to do that?!" Justin raised his voice just a little. "Did I ask you to make me a star? That was *your* dream. You didn't do all of that for *me*, you did all that shit for *yourself*! But that's not why I'm leaving. I'm leaving because I don't love you. I'm leaving because I now know that . . . that I can't ever love you."

Justin took a deep breath.

"I think I'm gay! And from what I hear, so are you!"

Tasha brought her hand back and slapped Justin across his face with all her might.

"Who the fuck do you think you're talking to?! You can't talk to me like that, you bitch-ass motherfucker!"

Justin was too busy catching the sting from her blow and fighting the overwhelming urge to slap the shit out of her, too.

"Who is he?" she said, completely focusing on his gayness, not her own. "Who is the little faggot who turned your punk ass out? Who is it?"

But Justin had already tuned her out. He walked to the study, where his bag was packed and ready to go.

He had made his decision after he'd taken his shower that this would be his last day in this house. He had even called a swank hotel downtown where he had shot an ad campaign. The manager hooked him up with a comp room. Justin told him he would only need to stay there until he settled his affairs with Tasha and could find an apartment. The manager told him he could stay as long as he liked.

"My only request is that you try to make an appearance in our lounge area as often as possible," the manager said. "I want people to see you here. It makes us look good."

The manager had more than a business interest in Justin, who until now would never have considered such a thing. Justin was grateful for the little bit of favor he had.

Fuck Dorian, he thought. I don't need him.

Justin also figured that he didn't need Tasha, either. She would get over this and they would move on. And now he had options. He could keep modeling, as Darryl had suggested, with another agency. Justin knew things might be a bit strange at first, but he figured that this was what was best for Tasha.

He thought it was fairer to tell her everything, to get it out in the open, be honest, than to keep living this lie. He knew that for Darryl and Anne this was about something more, but for Justin it was about living out his truth and helping Tasha see the importance of that, too.

"This is for her own good," he kept saying to himself.

He was thinking of all that as the Baccarat ashtray narrowly missed his head.

Tasha wasn't taking this well at all. The ashtray hit the floor with a thud, inches from his foot. Before he could react, Tasha was on him like a banshee, wildly scratching and clawing at his arms and hands.

"You motherfucker!" she screamed. This was followed by a few inaudible grunts and a few more expletives as she began to tug at his bag. "You are *not* leaving me!"

Justin looked into her eyes and saw no signs of sanity. They were wild and unfocused. And she had that crazy-person's strength. He could barely hold on to his bag and he definitely couldn't struggle with his bag *and* open the door to leave.

I have to get out of here! Justin thought. He finally had to gather his own strength to get her off him, knocking her to the floor.

She jumped back up and leaped on him, wrapping her legs around him and pounding at his face and chest. Justin struggled to get her off again, but it was like fighting with an octopus—as soon as he got one of her arms off, the other grabbed on; as soon as he was able to pry off one of her legs, the other leg latched on. Justin grabbed hold of her shoulders and shook her with all his might, threw her to the floor, grabbed her again and threw her onto the couch before she could get her bearings. But like a woman possessed, she came back, rushing him. Like a running back, Justin met Tasha's head with a stiff arm as the heel of his palm sent her crashing back for the final time.

Tasha tried to shake off the cobwebs, but things were very cloudy and she was seeing double.

"You motherfucker!" she slurred as the door slammed behind him. "You're—you're going to pay for this!"

Chapter Twenty-seven

Tasha was sprawled on the marble in her bathroom, hugging the toilet. She couldn't stop vomiting. Her upset stomach was emotional, not physical. Tasha hadn't felt this way since she was eleven years old, getting sick while overhearing her father verbally abuse her mother. Right now, she wished she could just curl up on the floor and die.

Her tears were on automatic and she alternated between hysterical cries and dry heaves. She couldn't pull it together. She felt so empty. Her house was instantly too big for her. She felt as if she was in mourning.

Tasha had been dumped before. She had had a few men leave her. But it had been a while. She hadn't had anyone defy her, let alone leave her, since she'd become *the* Tasha Reynolds. No one dared to even cross her, at least not to her face.

The last person who'd tried, a young upstart model, was still spoken of in hushed tones. This model had tried to double-cross Tasha by taking jobs that another agent secured for her behind Tasha's back. When Tasha found out, not only was this young up-and-comer on the next thing smoking back to Indianapolis, but she was also never to be heard from again. She couldn't even get a job as a Playboy bunny. Tasha completely shut her down and spread a rumor that the model had herpes. That pretty much killed any swimsuit, Victoria's Secret, or any other sexy ad. The last thing the public wants to think about when looking at a beautiful woman is herpes.

But that model wasn't the only one to experience the wrath of Tasha. Everyone knew how nasty and vindictive she was. It was legendary. So most steered clear of her bad side.

Justin had stood boldly in front of her and basically given her the middle finger. It wasn't what Tasha ever expected . . . especially not from Justin. She was totally reeling.

It wasn't just Justin's leaving, it was the culmination of everything that was going on with Anne, too. She had lost friends, lovers, partners, and business associates all in a matter of days, and as she lay crying and heaving on the floor of her bathroom, she was in the process of losing herself.

She was consumed with making Justin pay. For what, exactly, she didn't know.

Betrayal? Well, she'd betrayed him. She knew that. Was it that he'd cheated? She had cheated, too. But Tasha justified it. Hers was different. She wasn't willing to leave him for Anne. It was just something that had happened. And even if it happened again,

Tasha had reasoned that it would never jeopardize her relationship with Justin. She wouldn't allow it to. She chose him. But he chose instead to leave her.

That was it. The humiliation of being *left. Soon, everyone will know. Everyone will know and I will be a laughingstock.* At least, that's what she thought. She couldn't bear to look weak or vulnerable. It would be bad for business.

Why couldn't he be like the rest of the cowards and the liars who stick around even while they're screwing around? Tasha thought. Why'd he have to be so fucking righteous?

But Tasha also knew that it was deeper than the appearances—although that was the biggest deal for her. It wasn't just how it looked to the world, it was how it felt *inside.*

She was crying on that floor, with an upset stomach, because when Justin walked out, he took a big part of Tasha with him—the part she was looking to find. The sensitive, loving, human part, leaving this shell on the bathroom floor.

And she hated not being in control.

For Tasha, control was the fuel that kept her going. Knowing that she could be a puppet master, pulling the strings and watching people jump and bow at her slightest whim. If she had that kind of control over anyone, she would have bet her fortune, her life, that it was Justin.

"Oh, you want to leave somebody?" Tasha said to herself, picking herself off the floor. "This will be the worst thing you ever did in your life!"

Tasha went to her phone to call her private detective first and then her lawyer. She had to make her charges stick—and then keep sticking it to Justin.

In her *mind's eye*

I should have hit him with that fucking ashtray, right upside that big head of his. He better know that I missed on purpose. I just wanted to get his attention, let him know how upset I was. But he didn't seem impressed. Leaving me? That fucker!

What happened to him? Who *happened to him? I need to find out who he's been fucking. I need to know who's been planting those ideas in his head. He's not smart enough to leave me on his own. Whatever faggot he was fucking put him up to this. I know it!*

He was fucking a man?! I can't even see all of that chocolate sexiness with his legs in the air, sucking some man's dick. I'm going to have my private detective follow him. I need to get his cell phone records. I have to know! Who has he been fucking?

And was he fucking me at the same time? Did he leave him, and with that man's come still on him, come home to me? He better not have brought home no nasty-ass disease. If I have something, I swear, I will have him killed. I swear I will. I might just kill him my fucking self!

I'm going to destroy him!

Oh my God! I cannot believe he left me. What now? What am I going to do now? I can't start over. I put so much into that little fucker that . . . what am I supposed to do? He was my hottest commodity, my biggest moneymaker.

I loved him. I still love him. And I hate him.

Why didn't I follow my head? I never mix business with pleasure. I must be slipping. But there was something so special about this one. I thought we could do it all and still be okay. How dumb.

Dumb! Dumb! Dumb!

And when people find out that my man was cheating on me with a man . . . are they going to find out? Oh, hell no! That can't happen. How can I stop people from finding out? No one can know what really happened. Hell, I don't even know what really happened. But it can't get out that this man left me for another man.

I am Tasha Reynolds. This could really mess me up. I will not be invincible anymore. If I let this young motherfucker fuck me over, others will think they can get away with it. I have to set an example. I have to make him suffer.

Then I have to get him to come back. But I need to show him who's boss first. I'm going to fuck with him—take away everything he likes, everything he loves. I have to find out who he's sleeping with and buy that fucking faggot off. Everybody has a price. That's too easy.

Now you're thinking, Tasha. All of this crying is shit, is messing up your eyes. You're going to be puffy around the eyes and you have to go into the office tomorrow and act like everything is okay. You have to act like everything is perfect.

I have to find another creative consultant. Katie Dougherty is a bad bitch. She's not Anne, but I can groom her into something better than Anne. And I can find another Justin somewhere out there. His leaving may be a blessing in disguise. Everybody is replaceable.

I can do some sort of search and get sponsors and make money—maybe even do a reality show around it. Come on, Tasha, think. Turn this shit around.

But how could he just leave like that? I mean, he was serious. I can't just let it go. I can't stop until he's on his knees begging me to take him back.

Oh, he will be begging *to come back here. He will be* begging.

Chapter Twenty-eight

Justin sat in the back of the tight, dank police car, fuming.

"I cannot believe that bitch had me arrested," he muttered under his breath. His face was swollen from where the officer had slammed him into the door of the squad car before shoving his head down to put him in the back. His wrists smarted from the cuffs having been put on too tight.

He was under arrest for auto theft. What was he going to do? He didn't have an attorney. The only attorneys he knew were Tasha's. Even the one she'd gotten for him to help him through his citizenship process wasn't *his* attorney.

How could Justin explain that the car was a gift? He had no proof. No papers. Everything was in her name.

He had never been inside a police station before. And being inside one, he never wanted to be here again. Being processed was even worse than anything he had seen on television. First came the awful photo. He wanted to take a picture like Kimora Lee Simmons. She looked fabulous. But he was too angry to think about the fallout—the mug shot showing up on TMZ's Web site within hours. So he took the regular grim photo. At least he didn't look crazy the way Rip Torn, Glen Campbell, Mel Gibson, and James Brown had looked in their mug shots. His was more like Frank Sinatra—serious, yet still handsome.

Then the fingerprinting, which was humiliating, as the officer harshly rolled each finger on the paper and handed him only one wipe to get the ink off.

Great, I'll have to walk around with this reminder for a while, Justin thought.

But the best was yet to come. He was placed in a holding cell with a dozen or so real criminals. He was told he would spend the night there, until he could see a judge the following day. Justin made up his mind that he wasn't going to talk to anyone, and if anyone tried to bother him, he might go crazy and actually kill someone.

He must have had that look, because no one bothered him. The next day, he saw the judge, who assigned him a public defender and set his bail at $50,000. He would have been deported if his citizenship hadn't already been granted—not that it couldn't be revoked. But in this country, you are still innocent until proven guilty.

Thank God for that, he thought.

He couldn't make the bail, so he would have to stay in jail until a trial date was set. He was moved from the holding cell to a cell by himself.

Jail. It was everything he had ever imagined, the stench of urine and feces. The dark, cold cell with the cotlike bed and its thin-as-a-cracker mattress. Justin had not slept at all the night before and he knew he wasn't going to sleep as long as he was in jail. There was no way he could sleep on that nasty, soiled, smelly bed. He missed his six-hundred-thread-count, crisp white sheets and comforter. He missed the scented candle that graced his nightstand and provided aromatherapy all night long. He missed his freedom.

As he sat on the hard bed, with his head resting on the cinder-block wall, he let his mind wander to the only place that could bring him comfort—the sugarcane fields of Jamaica, when things were so much simpler. The smells of that rich plant, with the sun, the Jamaica sun that, while it shined everywhere, seemed to belong to his island. For the first time since he had been in the States, he missed his home. He missed his grandmother, his mother, and even his father. But this was the first time he'd actually missed his country and questioned whether he should even have come to New York with Tasha.

He knew things were not going to get better. He was miserable.

Justin thought leaving Tasha would answer all of his questions. He believed it was the right thing to do. Honesty. Living a truthful life. Sure, he could have kept on lying and sneaking around. Dorian seemed content with that. It even excited Dorian to make love to Justin right under Tasha's nose. But Justin didn't like it.

At night when he lay in bed with Tasha and she snuggled up under him as she liked to do before falling asleep, pangs of guilt shot through his soul. When Tasha wanted to make love, he always performed, he always satisfied her, but *he* wasn't satisfied.

Justin felt empty and hollow and incomplete. So he had to leave. Had to. He lay there most nights staring at the ceiling. As he would this night. He knew he couldn't spend another night in jail. The pride that had prevented him from using his one phone call and calling someone gave way to misery. He broke down and asked to make his one call.

He would call Anne. He could trust her. She'd know what to do.

Chapter Twenty-nine

Anne sent Darryl down to pay Justin's bail. Justin couldn't wait to be processed, get back what few belongings he had, and hit the fresh air of freedom. The sun was out and it hurt his eyes. It seemed as if he had been in a dirty dungeon for two days. But Justin gladly embraced the burning sensation as he took in one full breath of air. It tasted so sweet. He hailed a cab and headed to his hotel, as he had planned two nights before. On his way there, he decided to stop at Starbucks and then walk the rest of the way.

He took a ten out of his wallet.

"Keep the change," he said to the cabbie for the seven-dollar ride across town.

The smell of chocolate-chunk cookies and fresh-brewed coffee tickled his nostrils as he walked in. He truly felt at home. He ordered his latte and handed the man behind the counter his card.

"Sorry, sir, your card has been declined," said the Starbucks worker.

Justin took back his MasterCard and pulled out his American Express. He rarely used it because it had to be paid off at the end of the month, and despite the kind of lifestyle he was leading, Justin was still very frugal. He had his indulgences, though. He liked nice watches, expensive scents, and he loved his Starbucks.

Since moving to New York, Justin had become addicted. He'd discovered the soy chai latte by accident when they'd screwed up his mocha order once, and it quickly became his drink du jour. He had to have at least one grande every day.

"Do you have another card?" said the Starbucks guy. "This one didn't go through, either."

Justin was embarrassed and confused. His chai latte was less than five bucks. He put his AmEx back in his wallet, left the latte on the counter, and stormed out of the store. Justin had spent his last ten dollars on the cab ride. He took his cell out of his pocket and tried to call the bank, only to find a recording saying his phone was "out of service."

"What the fuck?" Justin hissed through his teeth. But he knew.

Tasha.

This was turning into a big nightmare. Tasha was making sure that Justin faced one problem after the next. Justin had defied her. He'd had the audacity to leave her. Tasha had said she was going to make him pay. And, boy, had she.

It had started with the two nights in jail, arrested for stealing his *own* car—a car he'd earned. Before he became a citizen, he could drive in the United States with his international driver's license. He could work in the United States with his work visa and the Tasha Reynolds Agency's sponsorship. But he couldn't own a car, register it, and get it insured. It was the Lexus Tasha had bought with the money Justin made after his third major job. He had never imagined he would be in a position to lose everything, so he'd never bothered to put his car in his name.

Why would he need to? He was, after all, Justin Blakeman—the face, or rather the body, of Ralph Lauren's Polo sport line. It came with a billboard ad in Times Square, just as Tasha had promised when she'd lured him from Jamaica. His image was found in every magazine from *Vibe* to *Rolling Stone*.

He had even started getting offers for roles in music videos, which Tasha had been very selective about.

"We are building your brand," she kept telling him. "We can't let you just be everywhere. We can't have you overexposed, or worse, exposed in the wrong kinds of vehicles. Trust me."

Trust. That word was beginning to have so little meaning. What could he trust? He could trust that he was broke, with legal problems and no solution in sight. He didn't even have a working cell phone. It was officially war.

He changed his course from the trendy downtown hotel to the place he had called home. Justin walked every block with purpose until he arrived. The doorman didn't even notice him as he walked by. Why would he? Justin was a resident. He tried to collect himself as he waited for the elevator leading to their penthouse loft. He was angry.

But this had to be settled today.

Chapter Thirty

"Oh, I knew you'd be back," Tasha said, grinning as she let Justin in.

"What kind of fucking game are you playing?" Justin said, pushing by her to get into the loft. "That jail thing? Not cute. Now the credit cards and the cell phone. I could just . . ."

Justin stopped himself because what he wanted to do was grab her by the throat with one hand and just squeeze.

"Now, now. I told you that you couldn't just walk out," she said. "I told you that you would have to pay. Did that time in jail jog your emotions any? Did you come to your senses about leaving me?"

"Yes, I've come completely to my senses," Justin spit out. "I am definitely *not* coming back!"

"You will be back," she said. "You can't survive out there without me. You have nothing. You are nothing! I made you and now I'm breaking you. But if you apologize, we can forget all of this silliness. Don't you want your life back? Look, you can have your boy toy on the side. I don't mind. I understand."

"You should, you hypocrite!" Justin said.

"Hypocrite?" Tasha replied.

"Yeah, you keep throwing that in my face when you have a little secret of your own," he said. "At least I was man enough to tell you. You still haven't told me about your indiscretion. You are still running away from that. So sad, so pitiful."

"Sad and pitiful?" Tasha said. "You little fucker! You need to go get an AIDS test. You want to throw around your little barbs, but I didn't put *your* life at risk. You're going around screwing God knows who and still sleeping with me. You were still sleeping with me and Mr. Turn-out at the same time, weren't you?"

Justin was silent. He hadn't considered that. He used condoms and didn't engage in anything that he thought was risky. But he couldn't respond.

"Yeah, you go out and fuck some guy and come home and fuck me and everything's supposed to be okay?" Tasha said. "I'm not supposed to be mad? Have you had an AIDS test? Do you know for a fact that you aren't carrying some disease that you might have given me?! Have you?!"

Justin was still quiet.

"So I don't give a fuck if you can't buy yourself a pair of drawers!" she said. "I don't care if you're completely down and out."

Tasha was holding back tears. She was angry and heartbroken at the same time. Justin didn't know what to say. But somewhere inside he knew that this hurt act was yet another manipulation ploy.

"You want to talk about decency? At least I didn't bring home a potential disease. But I can forgive you," Tasha said, softening her voice and appearing to be vulnerable. "Come back and we can work this all out. I'll drop the charges and make everything right."

Justin thought about it. If she was so concerned that he'd brought her a disease, why would she want him back? It was crazy. It didn't make sense.

"You can't make anything right," Justin said. "Not when you're so, so wrong. I'd rather take my chances out there with nothing than here with you. You think you can control everything and everyone. Well, Tasha, you don't control me. I only came back to try to talk to you civilly, like an adult, like a human being. You know you're wrong. You know what you're doing is dead wrong. All you're doing is making me hate you. I will *never* come back to you!"

"Oh, we'll see about that!" Tasha said, picking up the phone.

"What are you doing?"

"Yes, I would like to report an assault." Tasha put on her frantic voice. It was an acting job that would make Halle Berry proud. "It's my boyfriend. Please send someone, quickly."

"You must be out of your fucking mind!" Justin couldn't believe it. "What are you doing? You know damned well I haven't touched you!"

Justin was shaking now. He knew he couldn't be there when

the cops arrived. But where was he going to go? He didn't want to go through another night in jail. He figured that if he was going to be taken out in cuffs, it might as well be for a good reason. He slapped Tasha. And it felt good.

"Bitch! You want to ruin my life," Justin said, slapping her again. "You think it's fun to play with somebody?"

Tasha started laughing, which made Justin even more furious. He grabbed her by her arms, hard.

"Shut the fuck up! Shut the fuck up!" he screamed.

He caught himself in midscream.

"You're not worth it!" he said. "I may go to jail, but I'm not going to give you the satisfaction of watching me completely lose it. You're the crazy one here. You may have this round, but please watch yourself, Tasha. Watch yourself."

As he was leaving the building, Tasha ran after him.

"Arrest that man!" she screamed. "He beat me!"

Justin found himself in cuffs and in the back of a police squad car again. This time he didn't care. All he saw was red. All he saw was revenge.

"I'm going to get that bitch!" Justin said. "I promise."

Chapter Thirty-one

Six months later

It had been more than six months since the Ice Queen had stripped Justin Blakeman down to nothing. She had him jailed twice, took everything he owned, and tried to ruin his life. For months Justin had to face the embarrassment of his public dressing-down. She'd even outed him—which spread across the internet like wildfire.

JUSTIN BLAKEMAN IN A GAY TRIANGLE! one headline read.

POLO PRINCE REALLY A QUEEN! read another of the seedier tabloid rags.

He was a laughingstock and a fool. Darryl had let him know, on more than one occasion, how he had been pimped by Tasha.

But Darryl also comforted him with the thought that Tasha would get her day, real soon.

"Without her bottom bitch, Miss Tasha will fall," Darryl said. "No disrespect to you. But you were her bottom bitch—you were her top money earner, the one she depended on. She may have made you feel like you needed her, but she needed you. Just watch."

Anne had bailed him out the second time. She went personally to the jail and sat with him at Starbucks and they discussed his future over lattes. She hired an attorney for him and started to help Justin put the pieces of his broken life back together. A bond was created that day because the two, driven by righteousness and revenge, had a common goal, a common mission. Justin was grateful.

Darryl and Anne saved Justin.

He was on the brink of losing not just his possessions, but also his mind. And they came along and gave him something he sorely needed—friendship and a purpose.

He enjoyed going with Anne to the park every day to walk her beautiful dog, Max. Justin enjoyed having dinner with Darryl and Anne. He loved cooking in her huge kitchen, which had never really been used before because Anne didn't cook. He also loved restaurant hopping, either with the two of them or just he and Anne themselves.

They turned into the Three Musketeers.

And while Justin knew that Darryl and Anne had ulterior motives for initially bringing him into the fold, they were completely honest and upfront about it. And anything based on genuine honesty can grow into something more, which it did. Theirs had blossomed into a genuine friendship, into genuine feelings.

Justin's personal life was filled with explorations. He became a semiregular at Arcade. It was a phase he was going through, where he needed the release, the anonymity, the lack of commitment and questions. It was seedy and sordid and dirty, but it was just what Justin needed. He passed no judgment on himself or anyone else.

His life was so simple and happy.

He was even able to explore his entire being and it felt wonderful.

"I don't think I want to model anymore," Justin told Anne one morning over breakfast.

She paused before responding. She wanted to think about his declaration and offer him a real response.

"Why not?" she asked finally.

"I don't think I ever wanted to model," he said. "It was something to do. I thought it would be fun and Tasha seemed to want it so much for me that I wanted to make her happy. But it's not me."

"I disagree with you," Anne said. "But tell me, what do you want to do?"

"I think I want to do more things behind the scenes, like doing some camera work," Justin said.

"Okay. Let's make a deal: Model for me for one year. If, after that year, you still don't want to do it, fine," Anne said. "During this year, I will show you the ropes—every part of the business—and you can make your decision based on experiences. How about that?"

"That's fair," Justin said. "I know I seem like I'm all over the place . . ."

"You're just finding your way," Anne said. "You're still young. Give yourself a break. You just came through some real traumatic stuff. I don't blame you for not wanting to go back to modeling.

But you have to make some money to get back in the game. And right now, you're still hot."

As a model, Justin was indeed still on fire. With Anne's connections and reputation, and Darryl's constant promotion, Justin started working nonstop again. Within a few months he had earned enough to buy his own new Lexus convertible. He was determined to get that car back, this time in his name. And he purchased a one-bedroom apartment on the Upper East Side. It wasn't a penthouse loft, but it was his—something nobody (but the bank, possibly) could take from him.

Darryl was a force in his own right and was able to secure some prospects and help Anne recruit some seasoned veterans to round out her stable. Quietly, they began to land big accounts—accounts that she and Tasha were competing for. More often than not, Anne would get the job, not Tasha.

The battle lines were drawn—Tasha on one side, Anne, Darryl, and Justin on the other. There was definitely strength in numbers.

Anne was able to assemble the Becker Agency. She not only had the touch, but the contacts, the experience, and the team to put together an agency to rival Tasha's. Actually, Anne's sights were not on Tasha.

"She's not my competition," Anne told Justin one evening. "I just want this to be the best."

Her concept was to make the models partners. They had ownership in the agency, therefore her success had a direct impact on their bank accounts. It was the kind of thing that attracted some of the top names in the business. That, and to work for the legendary Anne Becker, made her agency an instant success. She was respected throughout the industry, from the clients to the photographers to the models themselves. Anne's name was associated with excellence, fairness, and class.

Her first priority was putting Justin back on top. It wasn't as difficult as she had thought. Despite the scandal, anyone who had worked with him found Justin Blakeman to be a gentleman and a dream. Getting him work was easy. Restoring his reputation wasn't so easy. But in a twisted society, where scandal wasn't necessarily a bad thing, Justin immediately got work.

After that huge scandal with the rumors of sexual impropriety and the nasty divorce, Heather Mills, who was married to Paul McCartney, rose to new fame in *Dancing with the Stars*. She didn't win, but she was certainly a media darling. Back in the day, Hugh Grant got caught with a prostitute and his career took off. And Eddie Murphy was arrested for picking up a transsexual, then went through a nasty divorce, and managed to get nominated for an Oscar. Ellen DeGeneres came out of the closet and went on to battle Oprah for daytime talk-show queen. So Anne knew that Justin would survive because, ultimately, people in America love to see people get built up, knocked down, and come back again. Justin was a quintessential "Comeback Kid."

His first job was for French Connection UK. Justin loved their campaign: "FCUK You!" It was in your face and unapologetic and people loved seeing him represent that. The ad ran primarily downtown, with a billboard that went up on Houston, off Broadway.

There were still a few corporate clients who steered away, but Justin Blakeman was officially back. He turned it out at the Phat Farm fashion show that was televised on BET. The crowd hopped and hollered as he modeled a fox jacket over his shirtless body. All he did over that first six months was run and do crunches and lift. He was more chiseled than he had ever been. This led to an underwear contract with Joe Boxer.

Three of Tasha's other top models—including her top female, Mira, whose contract was up—came over to the Becker Agency.

In those six months, the Tasha Reynolds Agency went from the hottest modeling force in the business to struggling to keep up with the monthly nut.

Chapter Thirty-two

Justin was puzzled by Tasha's call.

"What the fuck does she want?" he asked himself.

He was tempted not to respond, to just ignore her. But she had gone to so much trouble to track him down. Besides, Justin wanted to look in her face. He wanted to hear her cry, "Uncle!"

Justin was sitting on the floor in his new, unfurnished apartment when his phone rang. It was Tasha. Justin couldn't imagine why the crazy bitch was calling him. He also didn't know how she'd managed to track him down.

Who gave her my number? he thought.

He was certain that she hated him. He was certain that she could smell his happiness and wanted to find a way to snatch it. He was too content. He had gotten too relaxed, too soon. Now he was back *en garde.* At the same time, he had a soft spot for her. She did do everything she'd said she would for him, even if it was all for herself.

He was mad at himself for giving her a one-minute reprieve. He was even madder at himself for allowing that woman to make him a prop in her life and just going along for the ride. He was still angry with her for doing it. And he knew that *she* was angry that she didn't get her way, that someone altered her plans.

It was a call Justin didn't want to answer. But he did.

Justin arrived at his former home looking and smelling like a million bucks.

"They say success is the best revenge," he said to himself before getting buzzed up to the familiar penthouse.

Justin liked the success variety of revenge. But the kind he and Anne and Darryl had orchestrated for Tasha was sweeter. They beat her at her own game and in her own backyard.

Justin smiled as he rode up to the penthouse. A few butterflies fluttered. He was nervous, or maybe just a little scared. He hadn't seen her or spoken with her in months. The legal case had been settled out of court. His lawyer was so good that Tasha was almost charged with filing a false claim and almost faced jail time. The lawyer even sued to get some of Justin's back pay and the trust that she had created on his behalf. All of this was done between lawyers.

But the energy was still present, very much so.

Tasha was waiting for him when the elevator opened. She, too, was dressed and smelled like a million bucks.

Touché, he thought as he gave her a friendly peck on the cheek, more out of habit than anything else.

"Come on in," she said in a melodic voice.

It was a far cry from their last conversation, when she was calling him every kind of fag she could think of and having him arrested for battery. He almost didn't beat that rap on the heels of the auto-theft charge. The judge almost denied him bail. But he was saved by the attorney Anne hired, who convinced the court that the charges were frivolous and vindictive.

"I'm glad you could make it," she said. "We have a lot to talk about."

Justin was quiet. He didn't trust it. He didn't trust her. He *couldn't* trust her. Looking around the penthouse was like looking at his entire life.

Over the last few months, Tasha had tried her best to destroy Justin. After he left, she tried to blacklist him within the business—making it nearly impossible for him to work, at least for anyone reputable. That was until the Becker Agency opened.

She didn't just cut off his credit cards and stop making payments on his Lexus until it was repossessed and have him arrested. She also tried to ruin his reputation. Material things could be regained, but a reputation was much more difficult to repair. If he thought about it long enough, he could get furious all over again. But he was in a good place—too good to go back to those toxic feelings.

Justin was so glad he had made the choice to leave. It was the best decision he had ever made. It was one of the first times in his life that he chose to make a decision not simply to please someone else. He made a decision for himself. Justin chose to be truthful, not just with Tasha but with himself.

Staying with Tasha would have been the easy choice. Yes, she was overbearing, bossy, and difficult. But he had mastered her mood swings and ego. He could have continued living out that lie. He could have kept up the front—as so many do. But he knew, in the long run, that that wouldn't be fair to Tasha. And it wouldn't be fair to him.

He was also pleased that he didn't make his decision for Dorian's sake, either. He didn't leave her for a man, as she had been telling people. Actually, he did leave her for another man, but that man was *him*.

It had been a rough time for Justin. For a moment, he wasn't sure if he would pull through it all. He *was* completely dependent upon Tasha. She had brought him from Jamaica and, while he was never destitute, he was at her mercy because she gave him everything—a home, a car, clothes, a career, fame. His own family hadn't disowned him, but going home now, with all of the controversy, was not an option.

Being gay in Jamaica was a death sentence. His safety was a factor, but he also didn't want to bring more shame onto his family. The Blakemans were prominent on the island. They were a proud family. It was bad enough that their Justin was now a known batty boy, but he wasn't about to compound the pain by being there every day, a constant reminder of that shame.

Justin spoke to his ma-ma every week. And as always, she was supportive. But in her tone, Justin could tell that even she didn't approve of what was going on. She wanted him to "just come home." But she also knew what he'd be facing.

"I love you, Jussy," she would say. "Please take care of yourself."

Justin was going to make a way for himself in the United

States. He was going to finish what Tasha had started. He was an American citizen now and he was going to make the best of that in his new country.

He was grateful that he'd applied, at Tasha's urging and against his better judgment. He'd actually appreciated taking the test and being sworn in with all of the others. It was a proud moment under the red, white, and blue flag when he got his certificate stating that he was an American. He would always be a Jamaican, until the day he died. But he was also an American and he was just as proud of that.

Justin had regained most of his life.

Now, coming to see Tasha was about closure for him—closing that ugly chapter . . . for good.

Maybe that's what she wanted, too. Maybe this invitation would be about forgiveness and moving on. Maybe they could avoid further scandal. Maybe it would all be settled tonight.

Maybe.

"Can I get you something to drink? A malta?" Tasha said, leading him to the couch in the living room.

Justin nodded. An ice-cold malta would really hit the spot. He was letting his guard down. It was feeling like it used to, like when he would come home and Tasha would get there first and put the malta on ice so that it would be so cold frost would form on the bottle. Justin never wanted a glass, he liked the feel of the bottle against his mouth as the strong, bittersweet coldness would sting the back of his throat, making him close his eyes to the sensation. Justin loved that.

He wanted to be totally comfortable as he wrapped his hands around the malta Tasha handed him, but he had an uneasy feeling.

What is she up to? he thought. What is she *really* up to?

He decided to break the ice, risking also breaking the mood and incurring the wrath of Tasha. "Okay, Tasha, I appreciate the hospitality, but I can't help but be confused."

"I know you must be," she said. "What am I up to, you're probably asking yourself. Well, Justin, I am proud of you. I see you have put it all together and are making it happen and I'm proud of you."

"Well, thank you," he said hesitantly, waiting for the "but . . ."

"I can't forget how badly you hurt me, though," she continued. "You hurt me really bad—probably the worst pain I've allowed myself to feel in quite some time. I wanted you to pay. I wanted you to feel the same pain."

"Well, you did a pretty good job of doling out pain yourself," Justin said, rubbing the scars she'd left on his arm. "Getting me arrested, that was pretty low. And canceling all of my jobs and getting my car repossessed, and—"

"Okay, okay . . ." Tasha butted in. "I didn't bring you here to rehash. We've been on that merry-go-round too many times. Let's get off and move forward. I have a proposition for you."

On the outside Tasha was calm and cool. On the inside the fury had started to boil again, like an egg in a pot of water after five minutes. It was bubbling and she was easily transported to that night when she thought she would lose her mind. The night she actually did lose her mind. She was feeling all of those feelings again. But she had to pull herself together. Because this was the moment when she had to regain her life.

Tasha had to stop herself and take a deep breath. She didn't want to go back to that place because that place would make her go into the kitchen, pull out the sharpest, longest knife, and come back and plunge it into the soft fleshy middle of Justin's throat, just below his Adam's apple.

"I have a proposition for you," she repeated, "and it's an offer that you can't refuse."

Uh-oh!

Sitting on the couch where they'd made love for the very first time—and many, many times after—and looking at this man who seemed to be even more perfect than he had ever been, Tasha beat back her murderous thoughts and was trying to beat back her desire. It was a strange mixture of hate, pain, and lust that had Tasha swooning.

Justin sat silently. His unshaven face made him look more rugged and sexy. He crossed his legs and didn't move.

"So I know you're wondering why I invited you here," Tasha said.

"Um, yeah," Justin said.

"Well, I think this has all gone far enough," Tasha said. "We have gone through so much. And it doesn't have to end this way."

"I couldn't agree with you more," said Justin. He was holding back so much. There was so much he wasn't saying.

"So I want to call a truce," she said. "I mean, I know we can't go back to where we began. It can't be like it was before. But it can't continue like this."

Justin didn't say anything. He took another sip of his malta and nodded in agreement. Tasha finally sat on the couch next to him and turned on the television.

"You know, you didn't have to leave like that," Tasha said. "We could have talked it out. You know, being in this business, I have to be open to different lifestyles. I understand the temptations and I know this was all new to you. Why didn't you come to me and talk about it? Why did you have to just walk out like—with all of the drama?"

"Drama? Me?" Justin said incredulously. "Okay, I'm going to let that one go, Miss Call-the-Cops-for-No-Reason. I didn't feel it was right to keep living here when I knew I wanted to be somewhere else. That wouldn't have been fair to you."

"What wasn't fair was leaving me and creating this big-ass scandal," Tasha spit out. "*That* was what was unnecessary. I'm all for a little sexual exploration. You could have just let me in on it. It might have been fun.

"I could even have strapped on a little something if that's what you wanted," Tasha said, getting real close to Justin, stroking his face.

He grabbed her hand.

"It wasn't about the sex," Justin said. "It's something else. Something I can't even explain. But that's why I had to leave. You know I've never been shy in the bedroom. If it was just about the sex, we could have worked that out."

"I still think we can work this out," Tasha said. "I want you to come back and work for me. Just work. I have jobs already lined up. We made a great team and we can make a fantastic team again."

"I'm pretty satisfied with my career," Justin said. "I know you've noticed that I'm doing pretty okay without you."

"You can do *so* much better," said Tasha, a bit stung by his retort. "I have a surprise for you that I think you'll enjoy."

Tasha got up from the couch.

"Where are you going?" Justin called out, but Tasha just ignored him and walked into the bedroom.

What the fuck is she up to now?

After a few minutes, Tasha called out to Justin from the bedroom. He was reluctant to move. He knew how forceful Tasha could be and he didn't want that kind of confrontation. She was really trying his gentle spirit.

"Oh, Justin," Tasha sang out again.

He walked into the huge bedroom and didn't see her, but the door to her master bathroom was open. He slowly walked to the threshold of the bathroom.

There, in the huge marble tub, was Tasha.

On the other end was Dorian.

"Come on in," Tasha said, beaming. "There's definitely room for one more."

Acknowledgments

To Mark Hilton Plummer, my media liaison. I thank you for specializing in the impossible.

To my friends and family for their undying love and support and understanding, especially my mother, Beverly.

To Pocket Books—especially Louise Burke—for enduring more than expected and standing behind this project with much courage.

To Mitchell Ivers, my editor, whose encouragement and guidance made the process pain-free and enjoyable.

To Karen Hunter. A book can save a life. I hope this novel does in the hearts and minds of readers what it has done in mine. Thank you!

About the Author

Jonathan Plummer is Terry McMillan's ex-husband. *Balancing Act* is his first novel. He is a stylist.

Karen Hunter is a Pulitzer Prize–winning journalist, a celebrated radio talk show host, and coauthor of numerous *New York Times* bestsellers, including *Confessions of a Video Vixen, On the Down Low,* and *Wendy's Got the Heat*. She is also an assistant professor in the Film & Media Department at Hunter College.